FACTASTIC

A LEGO® ADVENTURE IN THE REAL WORLD

SCHOLASTIC

Welcome, LEGO fans!

LEGO® Minifigures show you the world in a unique nonfiction program.

This book is part of a program of LEGO® nonfiction books, with something for all the family, at every age and stage. LEGO nonfiction books have amazing facts, beautiful real-world photos, and minifigures everywhere, leading the fun and discovery.

To find out about the books in the program, visit www.scholastic.com.

ISBN 978-1-338-03284-0

10 9 8 7 6 5 4 3 2 1   16 17 18 19 20

Printed in China   95
First edition, October 2016

As queen, I have many subjects, and so does this amazing book.

Our universe is incredible.

Let the LEGO minifigures share it with you.

And check out the epic building ideas.

ISS astronauts orbit the
Earth about 16 times every day.
They have given us truly amazing
pictures of planet Earth.

AURORA BOREALIS

American astronaut Scott Kelly filmed
this incredible view of the Aurora Borealis
from the International Space Station (ISS).
Streams of color shimmer across the sky
above the North Pole when electrically
charged particles from the Sun strike atoms
and molecules in Earth's atmosphere and
cause them to light up.

CONTENTS

> Meet the Romans on page 22. We ruled the world for 500 years.

> Find out which Native American inventions you use every day on page 34.

Fantastic facts pop up everywhere!

Bats can find food in total darkness. Hang out with us underground on page 94.

Right now, there are 2,000 thunderstorms on Earth. Read up on page 70.

Eureka! Just 92 elements make everything on Earth. Learn more on page 58.

Greet the geeks on page 104.

We're searching the universe to find new planets.

You don't say! We're searching the universe for intelligent life. Better read this book.

Beep beep!

Learning makes everyone a winner.

No clowning around, at the end of this book, you'll be filled with facts.

IT'S HISTORY

Step back in time with the LEGO® minifigures as they reveal how history was made. Meet some amazing people from the past who built pyramids, ruled empires, wore blingy crowns, sailed the world, AND ate chocolate.

13

Me Caveman. Me a rock star.

CAVE PEOPLE

Early, or prehistoric, humans lived in caves, hunted with clubs and stones, and liked to dabble in art. They had tough lives, especially since their neighbors were saber-toothed tigers! But their brains were large— and growing larger. Humans would have a great future.

The most important thing we did was discover fire.

MEET LUCY

This fossilized skeleton found in Ethiopia (and named Lucy) is about 3 million years old. It is the most ancient early human skeleton that has ever been found.

MINI PICS

What did you do today?

Oh, I smashed some rocks to make tools.

Then I made some new clothes with this animal skin. Oh, and built some animal traps. You?

I went clubbing.

WHAT'S FOR DINNER?

Scientists study prehistoric teeth to figure out what people ate. It turns out they munched on just about anything. Nuts, seeds, grasses, ferns, bugs, fruits, animal guts, and wild-bird eggs were all on the menu. They even ate papyrus (a tough plant later used to make paper)— so they might have eaten the menu, too!

Many early artists left their handprints on cave walls. A handy way to sign their art, perhaps?

CAVE PAINTING

▶ Prehistoric artists created paint by mixing ochre, ground-up rocks, and charcoal with animal fat.

▶ Paintings have been found all around the world. Most are similar, often featuring animals.

▶ Paintings of animals show lots of details, but humans are usually stick figures.

▶ In 1940, four teenagers found caves containing about 2,000 paintings in woods at Lascaux, France.

▶ More caves with more cave paintings are probably still out there, waiting to be found.

▶ No one knows why prehistoric people painted caves. To tell a story? Or just for art's sake?

2,500,000–1,400,000 BCE
The first knives appeared. They were really just rock flakes.

1,000,000 BCE
Use of fire—awesome! It was much easier to keep warm, cook, and work at night.

500,000–100,000 BCE
The first fashion—fur, leather, leaves, and grass were draped or tied around the body.

Me have facts ON head. Need IN head.

60,000 BCE
Island-hopping people in Southeast Asia made boats from logs.

30,000 BCE
Flutes made of mammoth tusks—music as well as art! Things were looking up!

3,500 BCE
Wheels! They made moving heavy loads wheel-y much easier.

Would you look at that? Cattle, birds, bears, cats, and even rhinos appeared on cave walls.

ANCIENT EGYPT

In about 3000 BCE, most people in the world were still living in caves and hitting each other over the head with clubs. Not in Egypt! Ancient Egyptians were busy writing, feasting, inventing, farming, boating, trading, conquering, and building pyramids. They were a truly awe-inspiring ancient civilization.

DESERT RIVER

Egypt would be a massive sand bowl in the northern Sahara desert if not for the Nile River. It floods every year, leaving behind a fertile valley. This flooding made the ancient Egyptians rich in food and water. About 95 percent of Egyptians today still live on the banks of the Nile.

GODS AND CATS

Ancient Egyptians worshipped more than 2,000 different gods and goddesses. One of them was the protective goddess Bastet, who was half cat and half woman—the original Catwoman! Cats were favored animals in ancient Egypt, so much so they were considered sacred.

How many blocks in the Great Pyramid? More than 2 million! Awesome.

FANTASTIC PHARAOHS

Pharaohs ruled in ancient Egypt. They were worshipped as gods, and everything they said was made a law. The pharaoh ran the empire, built temples, and planned the afterlife. No one was allowed to touch him, and people had to bow down on the floor upon meeting him.

BUILD IT!

BUILD A GOLD COFFIN (SARCOPHAGUS) AND SURROUND IT WITH

HIEROGLYPHS

Ancient Egyptians called their picture writing *medu netjer*, meaning "words of God." But it was the ancient Greek name that stuck: *hieroglyph*, or "sacred carving."

> The discovery of King Tut's tomb caused a sensation! The whole world went CRAZY for everything Egyptian.

IT'S A WONDER

Towering above the desert sands, the pyramids at Giza are one of the world's architectural wonders. More than 4,500 years old, they were built as tombs for the ancient Egyptian pharaohs.

The Great Pyramid of Giza was 3,675 LEGO® Minifigures high! That's 482 ft (147 m) tall.

> The Egyptians preserved, or mummified, the bodies of their dead so they would remain lifelike.

> I'm the first wrap star!

Ancient Egyptians believed that they needed their stuff to enjoy the afterlife. So they filled their tombs with treasures and goodies. They preserved their bodies as mummies, wrapped in bandages. Tomb builders added secret rooms to keep everything hidden. King Tutankhamen's mummy wasn't discovered until 1922, by British archaeologist Howard Carter.

KING TUT'S TOMB TREASURES

2 thrones

A golden mask

A solid gold coffin

Food and 30 jars of wine

Perfumes, oils, and ointments

Clothing made of the finest linen

Rings, necklaces, and other jewelry

Golden and jeweled chests full of treasure

Sandals with images of King Tut's enemies

139 ebony, ivory, silver, and gold walking sticks

MORE TREASURE!

MYSTIFYING
MUMMIES OF EGYPT

1. An Egyptian mummy was found with its tongue sticking out!

2. The mummy of Egyptian princess Henuttawy was packed so full that she burst her bandages.

3. Over 300,000 mummified cats were found at the temple to the Egyptian goddess Bastet.

4. One Egyptian mummy was found with two left legs!

5. Some mummies were completely covered by a thin layer of gold.

6. 3,000-year-old mummies have been found with hair and skin.

7. It took 70 days to make a mummy.

8. Here's an eye-opening fact: Pharaoh Ramses IV's mummy had fake eyeballs made from a pair of onions.

9. Many royal mummies have their arms crossed high on their chests.

10. Pharaoh Tutankhamen had a necklace made from glass produced by a meteor impact.

11. People in Victorian England would buy tickets to watch mummies being unwrapped.

12. Mummified snakes, shrews, birds, monkeys, and crocodiles have all been found.

Come on, mummy. We've all paid to see you unwrapped ...

It's going to take a while. Those bandages can be a mile long!

Arggh! I doubt I'm going to look that pretty!

Shhh!

FIVE MONSTER MYTHS FROM ANCIENT GREECE

Ancient Greek civilization lasted from the 8th century BCE until 146 BCE. Greek culture has had a huge influence on the world. Greek myths are the starting point for many world-famous stories. They tell of powerful gods and human heroes battling terrible monsters.

HERCULES

Hercules was the son of Zeus and a mortal woman. He angered the gods and was challenged to 12 tasks. He had to defeat many monsters, such as the Nemean lion and the deadly Stymphalian birds. The ferocious hydra, a nine-headed snake, almost got the better of him.

MEDUSA

Medusa was a beautiful human girl who greatly upset the goddess, Athena. Her hair was turned into snakes, her face became so terrible that anyone she looked at turned to stone. The hero Perseus defeated Medusa, and from her body sprang Pegasus, the winged horse.

SIRENS

The Sirens were part birds, part beautiful women who lured sailors to shipwreck with their beautiful songs. The hero Odysseus told his ship's crew to tie him to the mast so he could listen to the Sirens' song, though it almost drove him mad.

Many creatures in Greek myths were half human, half animal. I'm a faun-half man, half goat!

CYCLOPS

Polyphemus was a cyclops, a one-eyed giant. He shut the hero Odysseus in a cave. Polyphemus asked his name and Odysseus replied "Nobody." Odysseus attacked him and escaped. The cyclops shouted "Nobody hurt me."

MINOTAUR

The Minotaur had the head of a bull and the body of a man. King Minos built a huge labyrinth to keep him in. No one could find their way through the maze. The hero Theseus managed to navigate the paths, unraveling thread as he went. He defeated the Minotaur, then followed the wool back again.

Brave and powerful Hercules was the greatest of all Greek heroes!

Odysseus was greater! He defeated a bunch of monsters on his way home from the Trojan Wars. Including you!

Some gladiators fought with two swords at once!

I've got a banana!

At its height, the Roman Empire stretched from the Middle East to Britain. It had 140 emperors.

GREAT ROMAN EMPERORS

Julius Caesar was a general who wanted total power. He died in 44 BCE but the rise of the emperors had begun.

Augustus became the first emperor in 31 BCE. He built up the army, roads, and Rome's forum or central square.

Trajan ruled from 98 CE. He made the empire bigger and much richer and put up some amazing buildings.

BUILD IT!

BUILD A GLADIATORS' ARENA, COMPLETE   WITH ARCHES TO MAKE

ANCIENT ROME

Rome was the capital city of a mighty empire lasting around 500 years from 31 BCE until 476 CE. On the one hand its citizens enjoyed fancy public baths, strolls in the forum, stone newspapers, and great roads. On the other hand, they watched gladiators fight for entertainment... and had some crazy emperors!

THE COLOSSEUM

Up to 55,000 Roman spectators flocked through the 80 arches of the Colosseum to be entertained for the night. One favorite show was watching armed, and highly-trained gladiators fight. Some gladiators were slaves forced to fight, others were desperate for prize money and glory.

Gladiators were celebrities. Kids even made gladiator action figures from clay.

NOT SO GREAT

Nero (54 CE) was blamed for a huge fire that destroyed much of Rome. When he rebuilt, he took a huge plot of land for himself.

Commodus (180 CE) fancied himself as a tough gladiator. Of course, he cheated to make sure that he won!

Caligula (37 CE) declared war on a seashore and ordered soldiers to gather shells! He tried to give his horse a top job.

AN ENTRANCE.

THE VIKINGS

They came from Sweden, Denmark, and Norway and sailed, traded, and raided all over Europe between 700 and 1100. The Vikings were known as fearsome warriors, but they were also bold explorers, peaceful farmers, and they had a wonderful culture filled with legends and music.

LONGBOAT CONSTRUCTION

Vikings sailed the seas in longboats. These shallow ships were ideal for sailing rough seas and slipping through narrow harbors. They navigated by looking for landmarks such as islands and distant mountains and by watching birds and whales.

1 The keel
A longboat's keel (bottom) was carved, then held in place with wooden blocks.

2 The sides
Overlapping planks were carefully nailed together to make the sides of the boat.

3 The prow
A dragon's head was carved on the boat's prow (front). It often glinted with gold.

4 The mast
The mast was raised. Stones were added to keep the ship as stable as possible.

About 80 trees are needed to build a longboat. I'd better get chopping!

MINI PICS

I, Leif Eriksson, son of Erik the Red, hereby claim this land.

Grrr. We already live here.

I hoped for a welcome party.

I can give you a bear hug!

BUILD IT!

DESIGN A VIKING LONGBOAT, COMPLETE WITH A FANTASTIC

VIKING VILLAGES

Some Vikings spent many years at sea. Others settled abroad, marrying locals and setting up villages. There are Viking descendants in many parts of the world.

He only popped out for a loaf of bread and he's been gone eight years.

5 **A single square**

Finally, the sail was unfurled. Oarsmen had to bring their own trunks to sit on!

VIKING LEGENDS

The Vikings told many stories about gods, giants, trolls, and dragons. They were full of magic, adventure, trickery, and mischief. They described gods and goddesses living in a sky world called Asgard, and people living in Midgard (Middle-earth). A rainbow bridge linked Midgard with Asgard.

MAGICAL RUNESTONES

Vikings carved symbols, drawings, and letters called runes onto stones. These runestones marked property or told the tale of a big event.

I will become famous! The first person from Europe to reach this new land!

I can't bear it. Time for you to Leif!

Vikings had style. They took baths (usually on Saturdays), carried combs and bleached their hair.

BARK, BUG, and DIRT are Viking words!

ANIMAL'S HEAD ON THE BOAT'S PROW. SAIL ON!

ANCIENT CHINA

China was home to one of the most impressive civilizations of all time. Over thousands of years, the ancient Chinese developed a rich culture, dozens of amazing inventions, and one incredible wall!

Kung Fu is as old as China itself. People were often at war, and needed to defend themselves. Hai-ya!

WORLD-FAMOUS WALL
To keep out their great enemies, the ancient Chinese built a great wall. The Great Wall snakes across mountains, deserts, and grasslands for 13,170 miles (21,196 km). It took 2,000 years to build, starting in 221 BCE.

A GREAT CITY
First Emperor Qin (pronounced "Chin") gave China its name. Qin made Xi'an the first capital of China in 221 BCE. Xi'an was the starting point for the Silk Road, a famous trade route connecting China to the Western world.

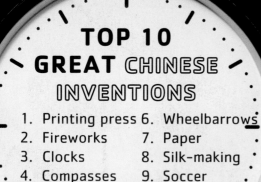

TOP 10 GREAT CHINESE INVENTIONS

1. Printing press
2. Fireworks
3. Clocks
4. Compasses
5. Kites
6. Wheelbarrows
7. Paper
8. Silk-making
9. Soccer
10. Tea

BUILD IT!

国

CHARACTER BUILDING

Chinese characters first appeared as symbols and pictures carved onto animal bones more than 3,000 years ago. These have evolved into the modern Chinese characters.

Colors have meaning in China. Red represents happiness and prosperity. Yellow is lucky.

TIME LINE

QIN'S TERRACOTTA ARMY

Qin ordered the creation of an entire army of clay statues to guard his tomb and show off his power. Some 720,000 craftsmen worked on the enormous army of eight thousand life-size horsemen, archers, and soldiers.

Confucius said, "Wherever you go, go with all your heart!"

The army was buried for 2,000 years before farmers digging a well found it. Well, what a surprise!

8000–2205 BCE
Early Chinese settlers built villages.

2205–1574 BCE
The Xia became the first dynasty.

551 BCE
Confucius was born. This great philosopher helped shape Chinese society.

221 BCE
Qin Shi Huangdi linked existing walls to build the Great Wall.

210 BCE
Emperor Qin dies and is buried with his Terracotta Army.

1368–1644 CE
The Ming dynasty ruled. The Forbidden City was begun and it was a time of great cultural progress.

BUILD A WALL. INCLUDE TURRETS AND STAIRCASES!

Women sometimes trained and fought alongside male samurai.

THE WAY OF THE WARRIOR

For more than 700 years, shoguns ruled ancient Japan, supreme commanders of the elite warriors, the samurai. The samurai came to follow a code called the "bushido" or "way of the warrior." Fierce loyalty was all-important but also learning, good behavior, and not being concerned with material things. Here samurai general Minamoto Yoshitsune dictates a letter to the shogun to ask for his forgiveness after losing a battle.

ROYAL RULERS

History has seen some all-powerful kings, queens, and emperors. There have been good, bad, and really rotten rulers, with splendid palaces and courts full of colorful characters. Even now, in Europe, there are 10 reigning royal families. Queen Elizabeth II is the queen of 16 countries!

When is a piece of wood like a king? When it's a ruler!

Who dares to challenge me?

I just wanted you to pass the ketchup ...

TOP ROYAL PALACES

Buckingham Palace, England
Principal home of Elizabeth II.

Palace of Versailles, France
Fantastic home of the Sun King, Louis XIV.

Pena National Palace, Portugal
Built high in the Sintra mountains.

Amalienborg
Home to the Danish royal family—has four identical buildings.

Mysore Palace, India
Built by the local royal family, the Wodeyars.

Grand Palace Bangkok
One of the most popuar tourist attractions in Thailand.

Forbidden City, China
Home to Chinese emperors for about 500 years.

Neuschwanstein Castle
A fairy-tale castle built by a shy king of Bavaria in the 19th century.

BUILD IT!

BUILD A SPECTACULAR ROYAL PALACE FOR A QUEEN OR KING.

Five fierce and famous rulers

Suleiman 1 (ruled 1520–1566) Suleiman led the Ottoman Empire of modern-day Turkey to the height of its power. Known as fair and wise, he was an epic poet.

Elizabeth 1 (ruled 1559–1603) Only the third queen of England to rule in her own right. Elizabeth forged a strong nation with great culture.

Gustav II Adolf (ruled 1611–1632) Nicknamed "the lion from the North," Gustav was a military genius who made Sweden into a modern power.

King Louis XIV (ruled 1643–1715) Known as the Sun King, Louis was King of France for 72 years. France became the most successful country in Europe.

Peter the Great (ruled 1682–1725) Known as the Tsar, Peter changed Russian life, from creating a tech-savvy navy to founding St. Petersburg.

INCREDIBLE CROWN

The Imperial State Crown belongs to Elizabeth II. It has over 3,000 gems including a 317-carat diamond. To get the diamond to London, detectives pretended it was on a steamboat while really sending it as a parcel in a plain box.

In 1845, the Imperial State Crown fell off a cushion and broke! The gems were put in a new setting in 1937.

ETIQUETTE

Etiquette, or social rules, were very important in royal courts. French King Louis XIV had very strict codes—not following them was a crime! To stay on a king's good side, follow these simple rules:

1. Never knock on the king's door—just gently scratch.

2. Always address the king as "Your Royal Highness."

3. Never cross your legs in public.

4. A lady must never hold hands with a gentleman.

5. Never turn your back on someone with higher status!

6. When the king wakes, everyone must be fully dressed.

AZTECS AND INCAS

Two incredible empires dominated Central and South America between the 13th and 16th centuries, though they never met. Some of their most beautiful buildings and fantastic treasures can still be seen today. Best of all, the Aztecs were big hot chocolate drinkers and ate corn tortillas with everything!

QUETZALCOATL
The god of knowledge and learning.

THE AZTECS

Tenochtitlan (now Mexico City) was the heart of the Aztec empire. The Aztecs were great warriors; every boy trained to be a soldier. They wore animals helmets, like this eagle, to show rank.

GREAT PYRAMIDS

The Aztecs worshiped around 200 gods. They built tall pyramids to honor them that reached to the skies. The Acatitlan temple was dedicated to the gods of the sun and the rain.

> Nobody ate chocolate back then, they only drank it.

> Argghh! Hot chili with chocolate! That's no treat!

OLD **HOT** CHOCOLATE

The cacao tree grows in the rainforest of Central America. Chocolate comes from its seeds. The Aztec emperor Montezuma II drank 50 cups a day!

MONTEZUMA'S BREW

1. Cacao beans were roasted and ground to a paste.
2. Water and maize flour were added. 3. Vanilla and really HOT CHILI PEPPERS were added. 4. The drink was poured back and forth from cup to pot until frothy!

OLD TIME

GODS AND GODDESSES

TLALOC
The rain god.

TONATIUH
The god of the Sun.

CENTEOTL
Goddess of the Maize, the most important food.

CHALCHIUHTLICUE
Goddess of water and all aquatic elements.

THE INCAS

The great Inca Empire thrived in the snow-capped Andes mountain range. Machu Picchu was an estate built for an emperor in Peru. The ruins are so remote that it was not discovered by Europeans until the 20th century. There were houses, temples, and terraces for growing food.

The Inca emperor Atahualpa had a throne of solid gold. He was sitting on a gold mine!

THE END OF THE EMPIRES

By the end of the 15th century, stories of cities of gold spread through Europe. The Conquistadors from Spain and Portugal set out to claim the riches. They defeated the Aztec and Inca empires and took over the whole of Central and South America.

TIME LINE

1200s
In South America, tribes across the Andes Mountains unite under a ruler called the Inca.

1325 CE
In Central America, the Aztecs build the city of Tenochtitlan in the middle of a lake.

1438 CE
The ruling Inca, Pachacuti Yupanqui, begins conquests that lead to a mighty empire.

1440 CE
Montezuma I leads the Aztecs, expanding their empire across Central America.

Young Aztecs became warriors at the age of 17.

1450 CE
Machu Picchu is built. The Inca empire now stretches 2,000 miles down the Pacific Coast.

1519 CE
The Spanish Conquistador, Hernán Cortés, arrives in Tenochtitlan. By 1522 he has defeated the Aztecs.

1532 CE
The Conquistador Pizarro and his army defeat the Inca Empire (but they missed Machu Picchu!).

FIVE AWESOME THINGS FROM THE NATIVE AMERICANS

People have lived in the Americas for thousands of years, from the freezing Arctic, through the Great Plains of the United States, all the way to the rain forests of South America. Native American cultures have introduced a host of things that are used right around the world, every day.

KAYAKS

The Inuit people of the Arctic were using kayaks from around 4,000 years ago. Early kayaks were made of driftwood. They were one-person boats designed to stay up in rough water.

TOBOGGANS

The native people of northern Canada built a nobugidaban—a word meaning "flat" and "drag." We call it a toboggan. Nobugidabans were made from slats of wood bent into a shape like the letter J.

LACROSSE

Lacrosse was one of the many varieties of stick and ball games played by Native Americans, especially in the eastern part of North America. It was played with a ball, which was caught with curved rackets with a net on one end. The stick used by the Iroquois people is the one that we use today.

TEPEE

Native Americans of the Great Plains moved around a lot in search of food, so they needed portable houses. They built cone-shaped tents called tepees. These were warm and dry in winter and cool in the summer, and among the first mobile homes.

POPCORN

10,000 years ago, the South Americans grew a type of corn that exploded into a delicious snack. They have been popping corn ever since! The Aztecs used popcorn to adorn their headdresses and as an offering to their god of corn.

When you next wrap up in a warm ski jacket, think of an Inuit! They fashioned parkas by using lots of layers to trap warm air.

Native Americans wore some super-comfortable moccasins

There are seven rays on Lady Liberty's crown, one for each of the seven continents of the world.

STATUE OF LIBERTY

A statue called *Liberty Enlightening the World* was a gift of friendship from France to the United States. The French scuptor Frédéric-Auguste Bartholdi designed the statue with the help of Gustave Eiffel, designer of the Eiffel Tower in Paris. Liberty arrived in New York harbor in 1885. She stands near Ellis Island, the gateway to America for millions of immigrants in the first half of the 20th century. She is the world's largest copper statue, 111 feet 6 in (34 m) from heel to head.

JULY IV MDCCLXXVI

Ready for a good knight? See page 42.

Meet some of the boldest battlers ever on page 40.

I'm off to discover something on page 44.

HEROES

We've found out some factastic facts from history. Now let's meet some of the most colorful characters who made all that history happen. Let the LEGO®

Shiver your timbers on page 46.

Gallop on over to page 50, cowpoke. Yee-hah!

AND VILLAINS

minifigures show you who's who. You'll encounter mighty warriors, brave and loyal knights, dashing explorers, particularly peg-legged pirates, and cowboys at home on the range. They found a place in the history books, and in this one, too.

Go, go, Caesar! He's our leader!

MIGHTY WARRIORS

Who's the most fearsome fighter ever? Read on to find out more about history's great warriors. They built empires and battled bravely. Some even rode elephants.

JULIUS CAESAR

c.100–44 BCE

Home: Rome, Italy

Skills: A strong leader, skilled negotiator, and great with battlefield strategy

Bio: Julius Caesar was a Roman general whose victories expanded Rome's empire, including modern-day France and Belgium. He knew the name of everyone who fought for him, which made him a popular leader.

ALEXANDER THE GREAT

356–323 BCE

Home: Pella, Macedonia

Skills: Ambitious, a smart thinker, and a skilled politician with a big imagination

Bio: Alexander the Great became king of Macedonia when he was only 19. He built a massive empire that stretched from Greece to India.

TIMUR (AKA TAMERLANE)

1336 –1405

Home Samarkand, Uzbekistan

Skills: Brave, smart, and clever with battlefield strategy

Bio: Timur was one the greatest warriors of Eurasia (where Europe and Asia meet). He conquered lands from Turkey to India, and also loved art and culture.

Pssst . . . ninja warriors were secret spies.

We Spartans were among the bravest fighters in history.

Samurai means "those who serve," and we serve well.

All hail, Caesar! I came, I saw, I conquered.

Round one! Who is the mightiest of them all?

VENI, VIDI, VICI

4 things Genghis Khan did that weren't really bad

1. UNITED THE TRIBES OF MONGOLIA 2.BROUGHT CHINESE MEDICINE AND DOCTORS TO HIS PEOPLE 3. CREATED AN EARLY POSTAL SYSTEM TO SEND MESSAGES ACROSS HUGE AREAS 4. HELPED OPEN UP THE EAST TO THE WEST

> Genghis Khan, he's our man!

BOUDICCA

??–60

Home: Norfolk, England
Skills: Courage and bravery
Bio: A famous female warrior and queen of the Iceni tribe. When the Roman Empire was in charge in England, Boudicca led the people in a rebellion against it. She was defeated, but her bravery lived on in legend.

HANNIBAL

247–183 BCE

Home: Carthage (present-day Tunisia)
Skills: Resourcefulness and elephant riding
Bio: Hannibal started a war with the Roman Empire at the age of 26. He eventually advanced toward Rome, crossing the Alps on a herd of elephants.

ATTILA THE HUN

c. 406–453

Home: Pannonia (present-day Hungary)
Skills: Fierce and ruthless
Bio: Attila conquered a chunk of the Roman Empire from the Black Sea to the Mediterranean. His fearsome nickname was Flagellum Dei ("Scourge of God").

GENGHIS KHAN

c.1162–c.1227

Home: Lake Baikal, Mongolia
Skills: Strategy, spying, hands-free horse-riding
Bio: Founder and Great Khan of the Mongol Empire. Genghis conquered much of northeast Asia and China. He ruled over the largest empire the world has ever seen.

> Sorry, Caesar. There's none like the Hun.

> Boudicca was a warrior woman, too!

> I wish I had a fearsome nickname.

> These warriors became legends in their lifetimes.

SUPERSTAR EXPLORERS' ADVENTURES

1. In 629 CE, Chinese Buddhist monk Xuanzang takes an epic road trip to India to check if the Buddhist writings he had were right. It takes him 16 years.

2. In 1325, Muslim explorer Ibn Battuta begins his 75,000 mile (121,000 km), 30-year journey by foot and camel around Africa and Asia.

3. In 1492, Christopher Columbus is the first European to set foot in the Americas since the Vikings in 1000.

4. In 1557, the galleon, the *Golden Hind*, sets sail on its round-the-world voyage. Its captain is England's Sir Francis Drake.

5. In 1804, Meriwether Lewis and William Clark set off on a two-year trip across the United States by foot and boat, exploring and mapping as they go.

6. Americans Robert Peary and Matthew Henson and four Inuits are the first to reach the North Pole in 1909.

7. Norwegian Roald Amundsen was first to the South Pole, in 1911, and first to traverse the Northwest Passage between the Atlantic and Pacific.

8. In 1960, Jacques Piccard and Don Walsh reach the ocean's deepest point, 35,797 feet (10,911 m) down.

9. In 1961, Soviet cosmonaut Yuri Gagarin is the first person to travel to space. He flies all the way around the world.

Sir Francis Drake's ship, the *Golden Hind*.

Edmund Hillary and Tenzing Norgay were the first people to climb Everest.

Hillary was also part of the team that crossed Antarctica via the South Pole in 1958!

Barbara Hillary was the first African American woman to ski to both poles in 2011.

Ed Stafford, in 2010, was the first person to walk the length of the Amazon River. Steamy!

Michael Asher and Mariantonietta Peru were the first to cross the Sahara Desert, just using foot and camel, in 1987. Hot!

A pirate is a person who robs a ship at sea.

Quit squawking.

PIRATES AHOY!

Centuries ago, the only way to journey long distances was to travel by boat. But watch out—pirates sailed the seas, hoping to steal treasure and even ships!

GOLDEN AGE

Piracy has been around as long as ships have sailed. But during the Age of Exploration, pirates were everywhere, as ships loaded with treasure crossed the oceans. The era from 1650 to the 1730s became known as the Golden Age of Piracy.

THE JOLLY ROGER

How do you know a pirate ship may attack? The crew hoist a Jolly Roger flag. A popular flag was black with a skull and crossbones.

PIRATES HALL OF FAME

Meet some of the best-known (and most terrifying) pirates ever to sail the seas.

FRANCIS DRAKE (c.1540–1596)

Captured a haul of Spanish spices, gold, silver, and other valuable treasures in the Americas

BARTOLOMEU PORTUGUÊS (1600s)

Helped write the list of rules known in pirate lore as the Pirate Code

ROCK THE BRAZILIAN (c.1630–c.1671)

Pesky Dutch pirate who robbed treasure ships off the coast of Port Royal, Jamaica

FRANÇOIS L'OLONNAIS (c.1635–c.1668)

French pirate who plundered Spanish treasure ships sailing in the Carrbbean

BLACKBEARD (c.1680–1718)

In charge of four ships and a crew of 200 pirates, with a thick black beard and fearsome appearance

ANNE BONNY (c.1700–c.1782)

One of the few fearless female pirates at sea, this Irish American woman joined a pirate crew as a teenager

BUILD IT!   YOU THERE, LANDLUBBER! CREATE A PIRATE'S ISLAND LAIR,

GRUB'S UP

On a long voyage, food was scarce and a bit gross. Meat was often rotten and bread filled with tiny bugs called weevils.

Check your biscuits for weevils!

LIFE ON A PIRATE SHIP

Old sea dogs had to put up with a lot on a ship. They could spend months at a time at sea. Conditions were cramped, there was no way to get exercise, and the food options were limited.

Crow's nest

Foremast

Topsail

Bowsprit sail

You're under arrest, pirate! Now hand over that, erm, EMPTY, treasure chest . . . Oh, rats.

Mainsail

Don't mess with me, I've got a short fuse. So do my cannons.

Do you like my peg-leg pose?

Bowsprit

Mainmast

Anchor

COMPLETE WITH HIDDEN TREASURE.

AHOY! FIVE FIERCE JOBS ON A PIRATE SHIP

Listen up, me hearties! Life on a pirate ship wasn't all about sailing and stealing. There was plenty of work to do, too. From the captain down to the cabin boy, everyone on board had a job to help keep things shipshape.

SAILING MASTER

The sailing master was reponsible for the navigation of the ship. There weren't many good maps around so plotting a ship's course took a lot of guessing. If pirates captured a ship with an expert sailing master aboard, they often forced him to join their crew.

BOATSWAIN

The boatswain was in charge of the sails and rigging and swabbing (cleaning) the deck. He was also an expert at making complicated knots from rope.

CAPTAIN

You might imagine a pirate captain was all powerful on the ship , but in most cases that was not true. The pirates voted for a captain they looked up to. He was only fully in charge during a battle. At other times, the crew could replace him.

QUARTERMASTER

The captain's right-hand man was the quartermaster. He ran daily life, keeping everyone in line and sorting out any squabbles. He also organized the food and accounts on the ship.

The 'powder monkey's' job was to run the gunpowder from below deck to the cannons during a battle.

GUNNER

Boom! The gunner was in charge of firing the cannon. It was hardly a blast. Cannons were hot, smoky, and accidents were common. It took six pirates to aim, fire, and reload while the gunner gave the orders.

We've got the treasure! If we'd lost it, the crew would definitely have voted us off the top spot.

Where's the quartermaster? He's in charge of sorting out all the booty.

THE WILD WEST!

Criminy! The Wild West wasn't called "wild" for nothing! It was full of varmints—dangerous animals and notorious bandits. Throughout the 1800s, settlers moved to the western edge of the United States. They came to start new lives, but what they ALSO found was rip-roaring adventure.

I'm rounding up the bandit and I need your help.

WANTED

COWPOKES

With all the wide, open spaces in the West, there was plenty of room for raising cattle. Cowboys were in charge of rounding up the huge herds.

ROLLIN', ROLLIN', ROLLIN'

Many people came to the West on wagon trains, groups of covered wagons. They traveled for miles across trails, stopping only to sleep and eat.

DOWN AT THE FORT

To keep safe, western settlers build hundreds of forts. These protected homes and kept traders' goods safe.

FULL STEAM AHEAD!

In 1869, the Transcontinental Railroad made it faster and cheaper for people and goods to get to the West.

● BUILD IT!

HEY, COWPOKE! BUILD YOUR OWN WILD WEST TOWN AND KEEP

8 infamous outlaws and lawmen

1. BILLY THE KID 2. JESSE JAMES 3. BUTCH CASSIDY
4. BELLE STARR 5. WILLIAM "CURLY BILL" BROCIUS
6. DOC HOLLIDAY 7. WYATT EARP
8. PAT GARRETT

In the Wild West the lawmen were just as legendary as the outlaws. But they'll never catch me ...

WANTED

ONE BAD-MANNERED BANDIT
Wanted for crimes of horse-stealing and train-robbing.

REWARD OF $5,000.00
MOST WANTED IN THE WEST

BOOM TOWNS

Little towns sprung up all over the West. Settlers built trading posts, hotels, banks, mills, and jailhouses, connected by wooden boardwalks.

CALIFORNIA GOLD RUSH

People came from all over the world to try their luck at "prospecting"—looking for gold. The population of California grew so fast it was made a US state in 1850. When the gold ran out, many left, leaving ghost towns and tumbleweeds behind.

In 1848, a carpenter discovered gold nuggets in California. The rush was ON!

Gold nuggets

WHAT IN TARNATION!

If you want to get by in these parts, you'd better learn to speak the local lingo, cowpoke.

▶ **Howdy** Hello

▶ **Giddy up!** Get going

▶ **Dude** Someone not from the West

▶ **Ain't worth a hill o' beans** Worthless

▶ **Yellow belly** Coward

▶ **Vamoose** Leave quickly

▶ **Doggie** a cow

Polar explorers made many scientific discoveries. They were also great poets and painters.

POLAR HEROES

Norwegian Roald Amundsen and Englishman Robert Scott raced to reach the South Pole in freezing Antarctica in 1911, Scott sailing on his ship, the *Terra Nova* (pictured). Amundsen reached the pole on December 14, 1911. Scott arrived there on January 17, 1912. Stories of extreme hardship and heroism from the Antarctic journeys circulated around the world. They have inspired explorers ever since. People push themselves to the limit to find out more about our world—and beyond.

AWESOME

shaken by earthquakes, carved by rivers, and battered by
raging storms. And it still looks beautiful! Let's meet Earth,
the ultimate force of nature.

ROCKS AND MINERALS

Forming on or under the Earth's surface, rocks are hard, solid materials made from minerals. Our Earth is a rock-making machine. Rocks are created, then heated, squished, or worn away into new rocks. At the center of the Earth, rocks melt and the whole process starts again.

Earth rocks. Yeah!

ROCKS

All rocks belong to three groups based on how they form: sedimentary (in layers), igneous (volcanic), or metamorphic (changed by heat and pressure).

Pink granite

Peridotite

Conglomerat

Flint

Pumice

Migmatite

Lim

MINERALS

Most rocks are made from natural ingredients called minerals. Minerals form into solid shapes called crystals. There are more than 5,000 different kinds of mineral.

Dioptase

Iron

Copper

Silver

GEMS

The Earth's core is made from molten rock (it is hot enough there to melt rock). I'd better not hit rock bottom!

Some minerals are very rare, or have beautiful colors. These can be cut and polished into sparkling gems and made into jewelry. The rarest gems are extremely valuable.

Sapphire

Malachite

Tiger eye

Ruby

Topaz

Lapis lazuli

ULURU

Rising from the desert plain in the center of Australia, Uluru is the largest monolith (a really megabig rock) in the world. It is 2.2 miles (3.6 km) long. It extends several miles/km into the ground. No one knows exactly how far.

GOLD (Au) is expensive and rare. All the gold on the planet would make a cube with sides 66 feet (20 m) long.

ARSENIC (As) IS VERY POISONOUS. IT WAS ONCE USED TO MAKE A VIBRANT GREEN PAINT.

The ancient Egyptians were fascinated by glittering gold.

FLUORINE (symbol F) is one of the most explosive elements, But in small doses it's safe! It's found in toothpaste.

CHLORINE (CI) is a greenish-yellow gas that kills germs—including in swimming pools. When added to sodium it makes sodium chloride—salt.

Fact Attack

Iron (Fe) is super-strong, just like me. The Eiffel Tower is made of iron.

IT'S
ELEMENTAL

Everything on Earth is made of a mix of just 118 pure elements. There are 92 natural elements and 26 human-made ones.

CARBON (C) is the

FRANCIUM (Fr) is one of the rarest elements on the planet. It is believed that less than 1 ounce (28 g) exists on Earth.

CALCIUM (Ca)
We have 2.2 pounds (1 kg) of calcium in our bodies. It is essential for bones to grow. It is also used for making cement.

Time for a glass of milk!

HYDROGEN (H)
BY MASS 75% OF THE VISIBLE UNIVERSE IS HYDROGEN.

Stars shine because they are changing hydrogen to helium.

HELIUM (He)
Helium is so light that it can escape Earth's gravity. That's why balloons filled with helium float up.

SULFUR (S)
IS A YELLOW, ODORLESS ROCK. BUT WHEN MIXED WITH HYDROGEN IT SMELLS OF ROTTEN EGGS.

OXYGEN (O)
MAKES UP ABOUT 21% OF EARTH'S ATMOSPHERE.

Ooooo, I can float, too.

CURIUM (Cm)
IS SO RADIOACTIVE, IT GLOWS IN THE DARK.

NEON (Ne)
is a gas that glows when electricity passes through it.

most vital element of life. Humans are about 20% carbon.

GALLIUM (Ga)
is a metal that melts in your hand. Scientists trick colleagues by making forks out of it!

PLATINUM (Pt) is the most expensive metal in the world.

Those humans are made up of 28 elements. It can't be hard to make one. 1 spoon of sodium, 1 spoon of copper . . .

VOLCANOES

Hold on to your hard hats, Earth is blowing its top! When the pressure gets too much, volcanoes blast lava from Earth's boiling core high into the sky. The clouds of smoke and ash can be seen from space!

Come to Hawaii and check out the world's largest active volcano. Mauna Loa is 75 miles (120 km) wide!

MOLTEN MAGMA

Earth's surface is like a jigsaw puzzle of rocky plates that float on softer, jellylike rock. When two plates collide, rock melts to form magma, a red hot liquid rock. Sometimes, this bursts through Earth's surface. It's an eruption!

Right now, about 20 volcanoes are erupting somewhere in the world.

FIRE MOUNTAIN

Underground pools of magma build up and up until the pressure becomes too great. The magma is forced up through cracks, causing an eruption. Layers of hardened ash and lava cool around the crater, often creating a cone-shaped mountain called a stratovolcano.

ash cloud

layers of hardened ash and lava

lava

crater

main vent

magma pool, or chamber

MINI PICS

Stand aside! The volcano may blow its top!

There may be lava and smoke and ash!

● BUILD IT!

IMAGINE A SUPER-SIZED VOLCANO.

BOILING RED RIVER

Above ground, magma is called lava. It can be 12 times hotter than boiling water. It pours from a volcano at speeds of up to 60 miles per hour (96.6 kph), burning everything in its fiery path.

6 volcanic events to run away from . . . very fast!

1. LAHAR (MUDDY TORRENT OF VOLCANIC DEBRIS MIXED WITH SNOW OR WATER) 2. GEYSER (POWERFUL ERUPTION OF HOT WATER IN VOLCANIC AREAS) 3. ACID RAIN (CAUSED BY VOLCANIC GASES DISSOLVING IN WATER DROPLETS IN THE AIR) 4. VOG (LINGERING VOLCANIC SMOG) 5. TSUNAMI (HUGE OCEAN WAVES CAUSED BY ERUPTION OF UNDERSEA VOLCANO) 6. LIGHTNING STORMS (INSIDE ERUPTION CLOUD)

ISLAND INVENTOR

When a volcano erupts under the sea, the lava cools, hardens, and piles up. Eventually, the rock rises up out of the water, creating a volcanic island, such as those of the Galapagos or Indonesia.

EXPLOSIVE FACTS

Magma can reach 2,400°F (1,300°C).

Magma can form 60 miles (96 km) below ground. Magma chambers are not so deep.

The word *volcano* comes from the Roman god of fire, Vulcan.

Yellowstone National Park sits on a supervolcano.

There are volcanoes under icecaps in Iceland.

A supervolcano is capable of ejecting more than 240 cubic miles (1,000 km³) of materials in an eruption.

When Mount Vesuvius erupted in 79 CE, it buried the town of Pompeii in Italy. The ash preserved some people like mummies.

You're a bit late.

This is Mount Fuji in Japan. It last erupted 300 years ago!

I'm studying the volcano with sensors so we can warn everyone if there's a problem!

Oh! OK! Let's go put out a real fire!

NOW BUILD IT! USE RED AND ORANGE BRICKS TO MAKE LAVA FLOW.

EARTHQUAKES

Earth's crust is on the move. Little by little, huge blocks of crust called tectonic plates collide or separate, causing earthquakes, volcanoes, and tsunamis. Most earthquakes are mild tremors, but very occasionally, they are strong enough to cause great damage.

> About 50 earthquakes of different strengths are detected every day.

FAULT LINES

Gigantic plates of rock make up the jigsaw puzzle of Earth's surface. The plates are constantly moving —about 1 inch (2.5 cm) each year. The plates meet along fault lines, but they don't slide easily past each other. They push and shove, and pressure builds and builds until it has to be released, shaking the ground as an earthquake.

THREE TYPES OF MOVEMENT ALONG FAULTS

Normal fault:
hanging block drops

Strike-slip fault:
blocks move sideways

Reverse fault:
hanging block moves up

MAP SHOWING VOLCANO/EARTHQUAKE SITES AROUND THE WORLD

earthquakes occur along the Ring of Fire

Pacific Ocean

Fault lines frame the Pacific Ocean, and it is here that 90 percent of all earthquakes occur. This circle of seismic activity is nicknamed the Ring of Fire because it is home to 452 volcanoes.

SEISMIC STUDIES

Seismologists study earthquakes. They use seismographs to measure ground movements too tiny for humans to feel. They try to predict the time, location, and magnitude of quakes.

> Some people think that birds and other animals can predict a quake!

SAN ANDREAS FAULT

This 800-mile (1,287 km) sleeping giant in California, US, is capable of quakes above magnitude 8 on the Richter Scale.

> Earthquakes are snow joke for mountain folk like me. They cause landslides and avalanches.

1. VALDIVIA, CHILE, MAY 22, 1960: MAGNITUDE 9.5 ON RICHTER SCALE, MOST POWERFUL QUAKE SINCE 1900 2. ALASKA, US, MARCH 28, 1964: MAGNITUDE 9.2, MOST POWERFUL QUAKE IN US HISTORY 3. HONSHU, JAPAN, MARCH 11, 2011: MAGNITUDE 9.0, TRIGGERED A TSUNAMI 4. TANGSHAN, CHINA, JULY 28, 1976: MAGNITUDE 7.5, STRUCK A DENSELY POPULATED AREA 5. HAITI, JANUARY 12, 2010: MAGNITUDE 7.0

> My top tip: don't make top-heavy buildings. Heavy roofs topple easily in a quake.

TOUGH TOWERS

A dizzying 2,080 feet (634 m) tall, the Skytree towers over Tokyo. Japan lies in the Ring of Fire so this tower was specially built to resist quakes. It has a concrete shaft and oil-filled devices to absorb an earthquake's energy.

The fault is about 10 miles (16 km) deep.

GIANT WAVES OF DESTRUCTION

Tsunami means "harbor wave" in Japanese. It is a series of huge waves caused by an earthquake under the sea. On December 26, 2004, a quake in the Indian Ocean off the coast of Sumatra, Indonesia, triggered waves 100 feet (30 m) tall and caused destruction in 14 countries.

> Robots can help with rescue and recovery missions after a quake.

THE RICHTER SCALE

A scale that measures the strength of an earthquake.

2

3

MINOR

2.5 or less
Usually not felt, but can be recorded by seismograph

4

LIGHT

2.5 to 5.4
Often felt, but causes only minor damage

5

MODERATE

5.5 to 6
Slight damage to buildings

6

STRONG

6.1 to 6.9
May cause major damage In populated areas

7

MAJOR

7 to 7.9
Major earthquake causing serious damage

8

GREAT

8 or more
Especially destructive near its epicenter

MOUNTAINS

Mountains rise all over the world from Earth's rocky crust, on land and from under the ocean. The tallest form when two of Earth's plates collide, buckling up thousands of feet, dominating the landscape.

MAKING MOUNTAINS

Most mountains are fold mountains. They form where two plates push together. Fault block mountains form when faults or cracks in the Earth's crust force some materials up, some down, and blocks of rocks become stacked. Dome mountains form when melted rock underground pushes up. Volcanic mountains are formed after eruptions, when the lava cools.

The Sierra Nevada mountains are fault block mountains.

Mount Fuji in Japan is a volcanic mountain.

Mount Everest is a fold mountain.

THE TOP OF THE WORLD

The summit of Mount Everest, in the Himalayas mountain range in Asia, is the highest point on Earth, at about 29,035 feet (8,850 m). New Zealander Edmund Hillary and Nepalese Tenzing Norgay were the first recorded people to reach the top, on May 29, 1953, after a climb up the southern face.

MINI PICS

Show me, oh great Yeti, how to conquer Everest.

RRRRRRRgh. I'm not a tour guide!

Take me to Everest base camp? I can climb from there.

RRRRRRRgh . . . oh, all right. Follow me.

10 things you might find inside a climber's backpack

1. HIGH-ALTITUDE STOVE 2. ICE AX 3. RIMLESS ANTI-FOG POLARIZED GOGGLES
4. CRAMPONS 5. CELL PHONE AND RADIO 6. A TABLET COMPUTER 7. ULTRALIGHT
TENT AND SLEEPING BAG 8. OXYGEN BOTTLES 9. RECOVERY DRINKS 10. IN 1953,
HILLARY AND NORGAY, THE FIRST PEOPLE TO CLIMB EVEREST, FUELED UP ON
TINNED FISH, LEMONADE, CHICKEN-NOODLE SOUP, APRICOTS, AND HOT TEA.

In 2008 Pemba Dorje climbed Mount Everest in 8 hours and 10 minutes, a world record.

MOUNTAIN WILDLIFE

▶ **Bumblebees**
In 2008, bumblebees were discovered on Mount Everest, 18,000 feet (5,486 m) above sea level! They are thought to be the highest-living insects ever.

▶ **Mountain goat**
The hooves of mountain goats have soft inner pads, like climbing shoes. The pads help them grip steep rocky surfaces.

▶ **Snow leopard**
This powerful big cat lives in the eastern Himalayas. It can leap the length of four cars in one bound, and its tail acts as a blanket.

▶ **Mountain gorilla**
High in the mountains of Central Africa, these gorillas keep warm with thick, shaggy fur.

5 MINUTES LATER

Everest grows 0.1576 inches (4 mm) a year. He'll never conquer my mountain!

Are we there Yeti?

Winds of 200 miles per hour (322 kph) and temperatures of -80°F (-62°C) —it's tough in the Himalayas. Unless you're a Yeti.

CLIMBERS NEED.

ADD A YETI'S CAVE IF YOU DARE!

RIVERS AND LAKES

Water is a force to be reckoned with. Rivers cut canyons and fill lakes, while icy glaciers bulldoze valleys. But without water, we'd be . . . well, thirsty. So, let's turn on the tap and go with the flow!

Nearly half of all fish species live in lakes and rivers.

The water in an estuary is brackish—salty and fresh. Not salty enough for me! Back to sea!

An estuary is where a river meets the sea.

EARTH-MOVING RIVERS

Rivers transport water to animals and plants. They also transport the land itself, powerful enough to wear down mountains and carry them to the sea. Every year, rivers deliver about 20 billion tons of materials to the ocean.

CARVING CANYONS

Stones tumbling in a river pummel the riverbed. Over thousands of years, the river digs deep valleys and canyons such as Arizona's Grand Canyon, which is more than one mile (1.6 km) deep.

SHAPING MOUNTAINS

Rivers of compacted ice, glaciers move slowly down mountains. Over thousands of years, they sculpt and carve the rock. They leave behind deep valleys, fjords, or rounded hollows that join together in a pointed peak, like the Matterhorn mountain in the Alps.

WATER CYCLE

Water is always being recycled, in the water cycle! Rain fills lakes and runs into rivers that empty into oceans. Rainwater also seeps underground and runs toward the sea. When water heats up at the surface, it evaporates, turning into water vapor. This rises into the sky and . . . makes rain!

THE WATER CYCLE

rain or snow falls

water vapor cools into clouds

water evaporates

water drains to the sea

Lake Superior, clean and clear

LAKES ARE GREAT . . .

. . . especially the Great Lakes! Michigan, Huron, Erie, Ontario, and Superior, together form the largest area of freshwater on the planet. They are so big, they can be seen from space.

Where do Great Lake ghosts live? Lake Eerie!

FOUR GREAT LAKE FACTS

There are six quadrillion gallons of water in the Great Lakes. That's 6,000,000,000,000,000.

Lake Erie and Lake Ontario are connected to the Niagara River and the Niagara Falls.

When French explorers discovered a vast inland sea, they called it *le lac supérieur*, meaning "upper lake."

Storms in the lakes can cause shipwrecks. But if you do fall in, there are 30,000 islands to swim toward. Goggles on!

TAP WATER TRIVIA

The water we drink is the same water the dinosaurs drank.

Water is cleaned and piped into homes from surface-water and underground reservoirs.

A person can live a month without food, but about one week without water. Get drinking!

Water doesn't hang around in your stomach. It leaves about five minutes after drinking, heading for the bladder.

Cold water is more dense than hot water, so it sinks. Ice floats—it is less dense than water.

A dripping tap can waste about 5 gallons (24 L) a day. Water is precious. Be waterwise and make a splash!

WILD, wEird, AND WACKY
WEATHER EVENTS

1. Snow rollers are created when a strong wind picks up a chunk of snow and rolls it into a giant ball. Ice work!

2. In 2010, Hungarians thought they were going hopping mad when a shower of frogs fell on them!

3. A severe hailstorm in Mississippi surprised locals by dropping a 6-by -8-inch (15-by-20-cm) gopher turtle!

4. In 2011, after major flooding in Ipswich, Australia, people were flabbergasted to see several sharks swimming down the road!

5. In 2010, giant hailstones as big as soccer balls—8 inches (20 cm) in diameter—fell in South Dakota.

6. Golf balls once fell from the skies in Florida. They were thought to have been picked up by a tornado.

7. In 2012, California experienced record-breaking boiling-hot rain!

8. In 2013, a 30-foot (9 m) wall of ice, an "ice tsunami," crept toward homes from a lake in Minnesota. It moved one foot (30 cm) per second. It partially buried the houses, shattering windows and doors.

70

9. Er Wang Dong in China is a cave with a cloud! It is so large that it has its own weather system.

10. Tornado Alley, US, sees more tornadoes each year than any other place on Earth. Once, in a single month, 758 tornadoes hit.

11. In 2015, mysterious orange snow fell in Russia. It is thought to have been colored by the red sand of the Sahara desert.

In a dry thunderstorm, there is no rain, but plenty of lightning and thunder. Striking!

Hey, stop stealing my thunder . . .

EXTREME WEATHER

Hurricanes, twisters, and blizzards all stir up a storm on Planet Earth. Let's find out what a tornado sounds like, why snow looks white, and just how hot a bolt of lightning is. Get ready for weather's wild side.

> A scientist who studies weather is called a meteorologist. I'm usually called, erm, crazy.

HOWLING HURRICANES

▶ A hurricane (also called a cyclone or typhoon) forms over tropical oceans.

▶ Moisture in the air warms up, rises, and condenses into large storm clouds.

▶ Strong winds circle upward around the hurricane's calm central area (the eye).

▶ Most hurricanes are huge—more than 300 miles (483 km) wide.

▶ Hurricanes are given a first name from a list made at the start of the hurricane season.

TERRIBLE TORNADOES

▶ Tornadoes are funnels of air that twist down from storm clouds and travel across the land as fast as a car.

▶ With winds that can spin at 300 miles per hour (483 kph), twisters sound like freight trains hurtling along.

▶ One thunderstorm can spawn several twisters, known as a tornado family.

▶ Tornadoes usually turn counter-clockwise in the Northern Hemisphere, but clockwise in the Southern Hemisphere.

Be careful over the United States. It has about 1,000 tornadoes every year.

The largest snowball fight had 7,681 people!

FREEZING FACTS

▶ A snowflake is a collection of tiny ice crystals, and a hailstone is a ball of ice. Sleet is a mix of rain and snow.

▶ The largest snowflake ever was the size of a pile of dinner plates!

▶ Snow is clear, not white. As the colors in light bounce through the ice crystals, they combine to appear white.

▶ A blizzard blows snow at more than 35 miles per hour (56 kph), while freezing rain coats everything with an icy glaze.

What's a tornado's favorite game? Twister.

FRIGHTENING LIGHTNING

▶ Lightning bolts are huge electrical charges created when ice and water inside storm clouds rub together.

▶ Thunder is the noise lightning makes. We see lightning before we hear it because light travels faster than sound.

▶ A lightning bolt is five times hotter than the surface of the Sun. Sizzle!

▶ There are more than 3 million flashes of lightning worldwide every day.

▶ Look out for lightning in sandstorms, volcanic eruptions, and tornadoes, too!

I dig dinosaurs. Find out how it's done on page 78.

I'm a forest fan. Let's go to the rainforest on page 80.

Meet some out-there animals on page 82. It's a zoo!

HOME ON EARTH

"There's no place like home," and that saying goes for the millions of living things on our planet. There's life on Earth everywhere, from the bottom of the oceans to the tops of the tallest mountains. Have an animal adventure with the LEGO® minifigures.

DINOSAURS

Velociraptor means "speedy thief." RUN!

For 160 million years, these incredible creatures ruled the world. Their fossils have been found on every continent. Dinosaur means "terrible lizard," but not all of them were terrible and none were lizards! Every year new dinos are discovered.

TRIASSIC PERIOD

250 to 200 MYA (million years ago).
There is only one supercontinent, called Pangaea, on Earth. The dinosaurs appear during this period.

Herrerasaurus

Plateosaurus

Coelophysis

JURASSIC PERIOD

199 to 145 MYA.
Pangaea starts to split apart. Dinosuars diversify, the giant sauropods appear.

Monolophosaurus

Barapasaurus

Stegosaurus

Compsognathus

CRETACEOUS PERIOD

145 to 65 MYA.
Dinosaurs are many and varied. Giant reptiles rule the seas and flying reptiles rule the skies. 65 million years ago, the big dinos suddenly disappear.

Psittacosaurus

Torosaurus

Carnotaurus

Oviraptor

BUILD IT!

IMAGINE YOU'RE A PALEONTOLOGIST WHO HAS DISCOVERED A NEW

Titanosaur is the largest dinosaur ever found; one fossil is 122 ft (37 m) long.

GRYPOSAURUS

This duck-billed dinosaur lived in Cretaceous times, about 76 million years ago. It was a big plant-eater, about 30 ft (9 m) long. It was first found by American fossil hunter, George Sternberg, in Alberta, Canada, in 1913. One hundred years later, it couldn't be a more exciting time in the discovery of dinosaur fossils. In 2014 alone, paleontologists found a giant raptor with a head like a chicken and a dinosaur with wings like a bat!

RAIN FOREST

Imagine exploring a hot, damp forest with trees as tall as 20-story buildings. All around, you hear the noise of hoots and howls, buzzes and screeches. Welcome to the tropical rain forest.

It's a jungle out there!

This place is crawling with animals, but the mighty Aztecs once made their home in the rain forests of central and southern Mexico.

WHY ARE THEY A BIG DEAL?

Rain forests produce about 25 percent of the oxygen that we breathe every day. The plants also absorb carbon dioxide (CO_2), cleaning the air. So take a deep breath and say thanks to—and protect—the rain forest.

A rain forest area the size of a soccer field has

1,500 FLOWERING PLANT SPECIES, 750 TREE SPECIES, 125 MAMMAL SPECIES, 400 BIRD SPECIES, 100 REPTILE SPECIES, 60 AMPHIBIAN SPECIES, 150 BUTTERFLY SPECIES.

The Amazon rain forest in South America is the largest rain forest in the world.

IN THE JUNGLE

▶ **Blue morpho** butterflies are so bright that pilots flying overhead can spot them.

▶ A river won't stop an **armadillo**. It can jump in, hold its breath for six minutes, and run across the bottom to the other side.

▶ The **jaguar**, a top predator, not only climbs trees but is also an expert swimmer. A jaguar attack? Cat-astrophic.

▶ The **poison dart frog** can be some of the most brilliant and beautiful colors on Earth.

▶ The **tree boa**'s babies are red, orange, or yellow. Like a sandwich left behind the sofa, many turn green as they age.

▶ The male **great hornbill** hides the female and their chicks inside a tree and feeds them through a tiny hole.

▶ Twisty vines called **lianas** can grow as thick as your leg.

▶ **Leafcutter ants** chomp up and take away huge slices of leaf to feed a crowd of millions.

Keep your leaf, Mr. Ant! We'll snack on chocolate, made from cacao beans from the rain forest.

RAIN FORESTS PROVIDE US WITH:

Oxygen	Chewing gum
Rubber	Coconut oil
Medicines	Shampoo
Coffee	Cinnamon
Chocolate	Cocoa butter
Cashew nuts	Vanilla

81

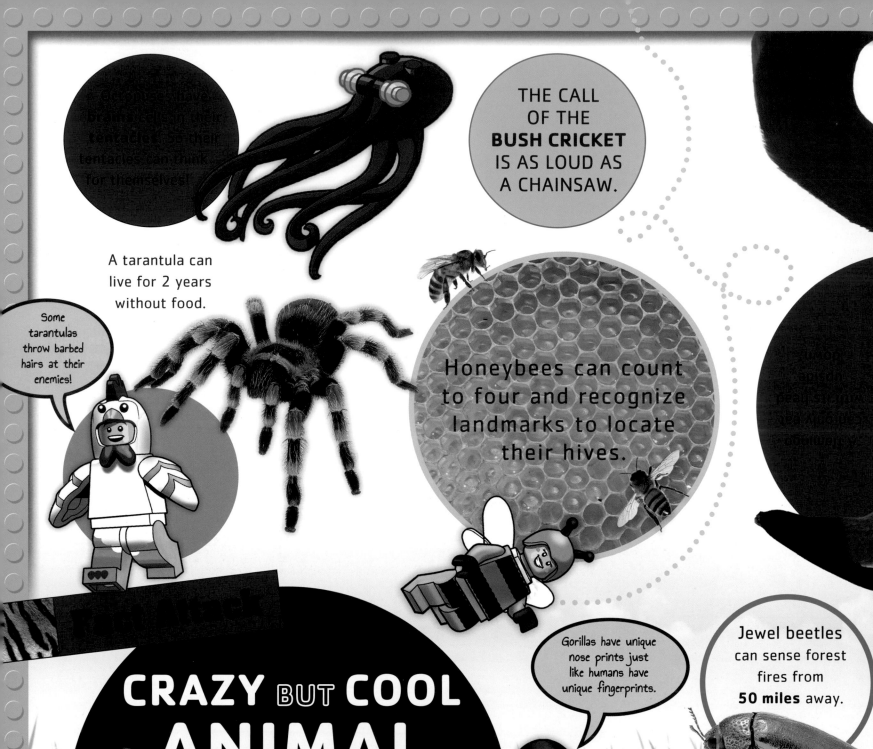

Octopuses have brains in their tentacles. So their tentacles can think for themselves!

THE CALL OF THE **BUSH CRICKET** IS AS LOUD AS A CHAINSAW.

A tarantula can live for 2 years without food.

Some tarantulas throw barbed hairs at their enemies!

Honeybees can count to four and recognize landmarks to locate their hives.

Gorillas have unique nose prints just like humans have unique fingerprints.

Jewel beetles can sense forest fires from **50 miles** away.

CRAZY BUT COOL ANIMAL FACTS

Proving why animals are endlessly interesting to find out about. Go figure!

Some

Sloths are so slow that algae grows on their fur.

A tarsier's **eyes** are each the **size** and **weight** of its brain.

Many lizards shed their tails when threatened by an enemy. The tail carries on wiggling!

Lizards' tails usually grow back again, sometimes in different colors!

THE STAR-NOSED MOLE HAS 22 TINY TRUNKS THAT SMELL AND FEEL.

ANTEATERS EAT **30,000** ANTS A DAY.

Houseflies hum in the key of "F."

The **Komodo dragon** can eat **80%** of its own body weight in one meal.

Female **lions** do almost all of the **hunting** for their family called a pride.

chameleons' tongues are longer than their bodies.

A cricket has ears on its knees.

A blue whale's heart is the size of a small car.

POLAR BEARS HAVE BLACK SKIN.

A spider's silk is one of the strongest materials on the planet.

SWAMP LIFE

About 6% of the world's land surface is swampy. Swamps filter groundwater, are havens for wildlife, and protect against flooding. So jump on an airboat for a swampy adventure and take a look at what lurks in the murk.

Swamp water is very clean. I wish all waterways were the same...

King cobras live in the swamps of Southern India. BTW What do you get if you cross a snake and a LEGO® builder? A boa constructor!

Hisssss-terical!

MINI PICS

So what brings you to the swamp, Lizard man?

I'm looking for a new habitat.

WELCOME TO THE SWAMP

BUILD IT!   CREATE A SWAMP, WITH AN AIRBOAT THAT CAN TAKE

SWAMP RECIPE

Marshes and swamps are both soggy spots. The difference is what grows there. Trees can grow in swamps while no woody plants grow in a marsh.

A swamp   A marsh

Ahoy there! Saltwater mangrove swamps along tropical coasts make it hard to land.

AT HOME IN A SWAMP

Alligators, frogs, and fish live in the nutrient-rich waters, with animals like birds and monkeys living in the trees above. Most are harmless to humans, but not so harmless to each other . . .

▶ A **mudskipper** is a fish-out-of-water. It mud-wrestles other skippers for its own patch of mud bank.

▶ A **heron** is a spear-fishing bird with lightning reflexes.

▶ The **crocodile** is king of the swamp. These prehistoric creatures are usually docile, unless they are hungry . . .

▶ A **snapping turtle** has a red tongue tip that looks like a worm. It lures curious fish toward its gaping jaws.

▶ The **green anaconda** is a giant snake that can reach 29 feet (8.8 m) long. Wild pigs, deer, and even jaguars better look out for this slick swimmer.

Swamps are excellent animal homes. There's plenty of water and lots to eat. And you'll love the neighbors.

What's that splash?

Err . . . looks like we have a tail-gator.

Yikes! See you later, alligator.

Airboats are powered by an air propeller and skim over shallow water. They can't reverse but they can go at 60 mph (96 kph).

YOU OVER LAND AND WATER. SPLASH!

85

Polar bears keep clean by swimming or rolling around in snow.

RULERS OF THE ICE

The largest land carnivores in the world roam the Arctic sea ice. Polar bears have fur thicker than any other bear, which even covers their feet. The bears are magnificent swimmers. A layer of blubber keeps them warm as they push through the water with front feet like oars. They don't stop. Polar bears have been tracked swimming 62 miles (100 km) without a break.

ATICACTASTIC FIVE

FIVE FEMALE EXPLORERS OF EARTH'S WILDEST PLACES

These five amazing women share a thirst for adventure. They have visited the farthest reaches of our planet—and beyond! Traveling by foot, kayak, submersible, or even spacecraft, they taught us much about Earth's wild places.

THE SUB-MARINER

Sylvia Earle is an American marine biologist. She has swam with humpback whales, discovered many new species, and even lived in an underwater lab. Having designed, and piloted deep-sea submarines, Sylvia now works to protect ocean habitats.

THE CONSERVATIONIST

Austrian Ida Pfeiffer (1797–1858) made two round-the-world trips collecting many important plant and animal specimens. For months at a time, she explored on her own. Pfeiffer wrote two best-selling books about her experiences.

AWESOME ADVENTURER

Helen Thayer, born in New Zealand in 1937, has walked across the Sahara and Gobi deserts, kayaked the Amazon River, climbed mountains, and even lived with wolves for six months. In 1988, she trekked to the North Pole with a dog called Charlie.

THE MOUNTAIN CLIMBER

Japanese climber Junko Tabei has climbed 69 mountain summits. In 1975, she became the first woman to reach the top of Mount Everest. She made a dangerous crawl across an icy ridge to reach her goal.

THE SPACE EXPLORER

American astronaut Mae Jemison soared to great heights on the space shuttle *Endeavour* in 1992. She was a Mission Specialist, performing several scientific experiments while in space. Mae orbited Earth 127 times during her 190-hour spaceflight!

In 1979, Sylvia Earle dived to a record 1,250 feet (381 m) wearing a special diving suit.

Junko Tabei was also the first woman to climb to the Seven Summits—on seven continents.

The desert keeps its secrets . . .

DESERT LIFE

Be they burning sand or icy plateau, deserts are definitely dry. Meet the hardy animals and plants that live there.

WHAT MAKES A DESERT?

To qualify as a desert, land must receive less than 10 inches (25 cm) of rain each year. And that's it! Deserts cover a third of Earth's land.

DESERT BLOOM!

Cactus plants are spiky water stores. Other desert plants have extra long roots to tap into water deep underground. Among the grains of sand, dormant seeds happily blow in the wind . . . until it rains. Then BLOOM! The desert is transformed.

DESERT RECORDS

Antarctica is the coldest desert. At the South Pole, the highest temperature ever recorded was a chilly 9.9°F (−12.3°C). The Gobi desert is classified as hot. But in winter, it can be −40°F (−40°C) making it the coldest hot desert. The Sahara is one of the hottest deserts with temperatures that can fry an egg— over 116.6°F (47°C).

Desert plants like jojoba make lush face creams. We ancient Egyptians have been using it for years. And look how beautiful we are . . .

BUILD IT!

BUILD A DUNE

WELCOME SIGHT

Oases, pools of water in the desert, form from underground water sources. Sand easily blows into water, so people often plant a protective ring of palms around oases.

AMAZING ANIMALS

Animals have developed ingenious ways to survive.

▶ The **thorny devil** is a lizard of the Australian Outback. Tiny channels between its thorny scales lead water to its mouth.

▶ The **sidewinder snake** moves in such a way that only two points of its body are in contact with the hot sand at a time.

▶ The **camel** is the "ship of the desert." It has long lashes and closeable nostrils to keep out sandstorms. Their wide feet act like snowshoes.

▶ The **African Pixie Frog** buries itself underground in a mucus membrane. It can stay like that for up to several years, until new rain wakes it up.

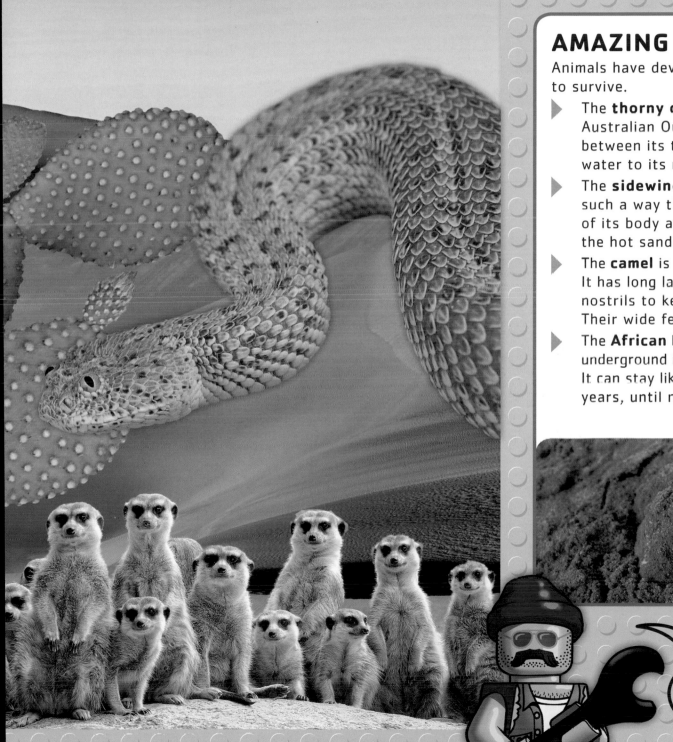

BUGGY WITH BIG WHEELS AND A ROLL CAGE.

CAVE LIFE

Slide down ropes into the deep, dank world of caves. Some animals visit; others spend their entire lives in the dark.

It's DEEP, man!

I'm off spelunking. Wanna come?

CAVE CREATURES

▶ The **olm salamander** swims in cave pools, blind, pale, with super senses, including the ability to sense electricity.

▶ **Crickets** have long legs and antennae to guide them through the dark. They're found in old mines as well as caves.

▶ Bracken Cave in Texas, US, has the largest **colony of bats** in the world. It's estimated that 20 million bats hang out there in the summer.

▶ When winter arrives, **North American black bears** hibernate in dens, made in caves or other sheltered places. They've eaten so much in the summer, they can live off stored body fat.

▶ Though usually pretty small, **giant cave spiders** can have legs more than 12 inches (30 cm) long.

Watch out for vampire bats! They feed on blood!

4 totally cavernous caves

1. IN THE **CAVE OF CRYSTALS,** MEXICO, THE CRYSTALS ARE BIGGER THAN A HOUSE. 2. THE **GLOWWORM CAVE IN** NEW ZEALAND IS FULL OF THOUSANDS OF WORMS THAT GLOW LIKE STARS. 3. SAY GOOD-BYE TO DAYLIGHT WHEN YOU ENTER THE **KRUBERA CAVE, GEORGIA.** IT'S THE DEEPEST IN THE WORLD AND STRETCHES OVER 1.2 MILES (2 KM) TOWARD THE EARTH'S CORE. 4. THE **SON DOONG CAVE** IN VIETNAM IS THE LARGEST KNOWN CAVE IN THE WORLD. IT IS FILLED WITH COUNTLESS WONDERS, INCLUDING 230-FEET-TALL (70 M) STALAGMITES.

Caves make good shelters from the hot sun as well as the icy rain and snow.

Not all early people lived in caves, though, especially if bears got there first.

Speleology is the name for the science of caves.

Potholing, caving or spelunking is the name for exploring caves for fun.

A stalactite hangs from the roof of a cave. It forms slowly, drip by drip, as dissolved minerals are deposited in tiny specks by the drips.

A stalagmite forms when dissolved minerals from drips build up on a cave floor.

The ocean is full of strange creatures. Starfish have no brains and no blood.

OCEAN LIFE

Earth's five, salty oceans—the Pacific, Atlantic, Indian, Southern, and Arctic—cover more than 70% of its surface. The weather on top and the currents beneath move water between oceans. One drop of water, in time, could travel around the world.

CORAL REEF

Coral is a living organism of polyps that grows in the ocean's sunlit zone. Coral attacks its food with stinging cells and gets its color from the algae that live inside it. Coral reefs are the most diverse ocean habitat providing food and homes for many sea creatures.

Giant brain coral

Jellyfish

Flying fish

Sunlit zone: 0–650 feet (200 m). Heat and light are in abundance. Colorful fish and coral reefs are found here. Plants live in this zone only.

Crab

Twilight zone: 650–3,300 feet (200–1,006 m). The light is dim in this zone. Many fish are silver-colored.

Squid

Sea spider

Cookiecutter shark

Dark zone: 3,300–13,000 feet (1,006–3,962 m). Say good-bye to sunlight. It's pitch dark. Many fish produce their own light.

Let's go to the dark zone. I want to find a dragonfish. It has teeth on its tongue!

Brittle star

FISH TALK

Fish don't have vocal cords but they can "talk." Some vibrate their muscles, some rattle their bones, and some gnash their teeth to communicate. They pop, hoot, croak, and bark.

8 record-breaking residents of the sea

1. FASTEST: THE SAILFISH AT 68 MPH (109 KPH) 2. BIGGEST: THE BLUE WHALE 100 FEET (30 M) LONG 3. MOST POISONOUS: THE BOX JELLYFISH 4. LARGEST PREDATORY FISH: THE GREAT WHITE SHARK 5. LONGEST BONY FISH: THE OARFISH CAN GROW TO 50 FEET (15 M) LONG 6. BIGGEST CRAB: JAPANESE SPIDER CRAB, 12 FEET (3.7 M) LONG 7. MOST NUMEROUS CREATURE: COPEPODS 8. MOST NUMEROUS FISH: THE BRISTLEMOUTH (A DEEP-SEA FISH)

Dolphin

Shark

Turtle

Tuna fish

Octopus

Sperm whale

Catshark

Krill

Watch where you swim. Some of the most poisonous creatures in the world live in the sea.

Sea star

Anglerfish

Viperfish

Abyssal zone: 13,000–20,000 feet (3,962–6,096 m). The water is just above freezing. Not much can survive because of the immense water pressure.

Tripod fish

Sea cucumber

Deep sea snail

DEEP-SEA LIFE

It's pitch dark and the pressure is immense. The water is only just above freezing, and the only food is fallout from above. What would live in the deep dark part of the ocean?

Watch out, the deep sea is full of creepy creatures like vampire squid, fang-tooth fish, and hairy crabs...

In February 2016, we heard the first ever sounds recorded from the depths of the Mariana Trench. It's a noisy place!

MARIANA TRENCH
The deepest part of Earth's oceans is in the Mariana Trench, in the Pacific Ocean. It is almost seven miles (11 km) deep. Only three people have ever been down to the bottom.

EXPLORING THE DEPTHS

Some parts of the ocean are as deep as Everest is high. Despite this, scientists have developed marine robots and high-tech submersibles that can explore the dark depths.

A 3-inch-thick (73.5 mm) thick titanium pressure hull keeps it from imploding.

The Shinkai 6500 is a Japanese submersible that can dive to 21,000 feet (6,400 m).

Two pilots and one researcher can operate within it.

MINI PICS

Hey! It's a shipwreck! I'll look for some lost treasure.

Huh? There's a light in there. Someone's got there first!

Arggh! It's a lantern shark that glows in the dark! I'm out of here!

BUILD IT!   MAKE A DEEP-SEA SUBMERSIBLE READY TO EXPLORE THE OCEAN DEPTHS.

BIOLUMINESCENCE

At 6,000 feet (1,829 m) below is a circus of extraordinary deep-sea creatures. Many produce light in their bodies, called bioluminescense, which they use for communication, finding food, and defense. The anglerfish has a bioluminescent lure to attract prey.

Scientists have explored only 1% of the ocean depths.

SHARK BITES
TO SINK YOUR TEETH INTO

1. Sharks are super smellers. A shark can sniff out a colony of seals up to 2 miles (3.2 km) away.

2. A shark loses about one tooth a week, but there are more behind it, waiting to pop in to place. Some sharks use up over 10,000 teeth in a lifetime.

3. Prehistoric shark Megalodon was a 60 feet (18 m) giant with teeth that were 7 inches (18 cm) long.

4. Almost 50 different kinds of shark have photophores, organs that give off light.

5. Statistically, bee stings are more dangerous to humans than shark bites.

6. Sharks don't really like the taste of people. They may bite them out of curiosity before spitting them out and finding something more delicious.

7. Although most sharks are gray or brown, some are pink, yellow, or blue.

8. After a big meal, a great white shark can go for two weeks or so without feeding again.

9. Sharks don't have bones. Instead, their skeletons are made of lightweight and flexible cartilage.

10. A great white shark gives birth to two to ten babies, called pups. Pups can swim right after they are born.

I'm the Ocean King, even though the sharks think they own the place.

Yes, sharks have a pretty bad reputation . . .

Man-munching monsters . . . You know the drill . . .

But only 20 of the 400 shark species attack people . . . and not mermaids.

So maybe that guy over there is number 19!

Greet the great geeks on page 104.

I ♥ my technology. See page 110.

Science can be messy. Find out why on page 107.

INVENTION

Imagine creating or thinking up something totally new. Something no one has ever built or thought of before. Your invention might be as simple as

There is an amazing new wave on page 108.

See some top tech on page 110.

Read about the rise of the robots on page 112.

AND DISCOVERY

a toothbrush with a built-in dispenser, or something that changes the lives of millions of people. First, though, you will need some inspiration. Let the minifigures introduce you to some of the greatest creators, discoveries, and inventions in history.

FIVE SUPER SCIENTISTS AND THE BEST IDEAS EVER!

Geek alert! Meet five of the greatest scientists of all time. They had big brains and even bigger ideas about how to explain some of the trickiest stuff in the universe, from gravity to space and time.

GALILEO GALILEI
(1564–1642)
Italian brainiac Galileo Galilei built his own telescope without ever seeing one. He explored the night sky, discovering the four largest moons of Jupiter, mountains and valleys on the surface of our moon, sunspots, and the movements of Venus.

ARCHIMEDES
(c.290–212 BCE)
This ancient Greek genius explained how machines work, from levers and pulleys to a screw to raise water. He worked out pi (the ratio of the circumference of a circle to its diameter) to 99.9% accuracy.

ISAAC NEWTON
(1643–1727)
Inspired by watching an apple fall from a tree, Issac Newton explained that gravity is everywhere. He was famous for his three laws of motion, showing how forces cause an object to move. He also developed the branch of math known as calculus.

MARIE CURIE

(1867–1934)

Polish chemist Marie Curie discovered two new chemical elements, polonium and radium. These elements helped medical scientists develop X-ray machines and fight cancer. In 1911, Curie became the first person to win two Nobel prizes, the top award for scientists and other thinkers.

ALBERT EINSTIEN

(1879–1955)

German-born physicist Albert Einstein's Theory of Relativity explained many mysteries of the universe and showed how space and time are linked. Einstein wrote a famous equation: $E = mc^2$. E is an object's energy, m its mass, and c is the speed of light.

$E = mc^2$

Science is amazing! All that knowledge we get from testing out our ideas can help us to explain everything in the universe.

Maybe that explains why you have a particularly large head.

10 HELPFUL
INVENTIONS

1. Fireworks were invented more than 2,000 years ago when a cook in China was experimenting with kitchen ingredients.

2. The oldest documented artificial human body part is a toe made of wood and leather. It was found attached to an ancient Egyptian mummy.

3. Restaurant-owner George Crum invented potato chips in 1853. His customers kept saying that the fried potatoes weren't thin enough . . .

4. Make it rain! In 2014, scientists worked out a way to fire rain-making laser beams into clouds. The beams may also cause lightning.

5. In 1931, Goventosa de Udine built a motorized monowheel—a motorbike with one huge wheel encircling the driver. It could travel up to 93 miles per hour (150 kph).

6. Three students in England invented a motorized bath in the 1960s. It had three wheels, a license plate, and a rubber duck horn.

7. Get off my lunch! An anti-theft lunch bag appeared in 2008. Mold printed on the bag made the sandwich inside look . . . moldy!

8. An invisibility cloak was revealed in 2011. It used a mineral that bends light rays, tricking the eyes to create an illusion of invisibility.

9. In 2013 a five-year-old invented an all-in-one toothbrush, with a toothpaste dispenser built in. Just squeeze. No mess and no lid!

10. James Stuart Blackton invented animated movies! His 1906 short animation, *Humorous Phases of Funny Faces*, was the first to be made using a standard film format.

The scientist Albert Einstein predicted the existence of gravitational waves in 1936.

GRAVITATIONAL WAVES

Sometimes there are discoveries made in science that change the way we think about the universe. In 2016, scientists detected gravitational waves for the first time. These were ripples in the universe made when two black holes collided and sent out waves so powerful they squeezed and stretched space and time. Now we have a new way to explore the universe.

INVENTION TIME LINE

When there is a tricky problem that needs solving, people invent things. Whether it's a way of working, a product, or a machine, inventions help us to do all kinds of things. Job done!

> Cave people invented using natural stuff like stone, wood, and rocks.

EARLY INVENTIONS

Many inventions don't just appear, they change through history. Sometimes inventions are made by turning existing ideas into even better ones.

c. 1,000,000 BCE Cave people invented ways to make fire.

c. 3500 BCE The invention of the wheel got people going.

2000 BCE The Babylonians invented the number zero.

140 BCE Paper is invented in China.

WHAT'S NEXT?

A good idea doesn't always lead to a great invention. A new gadget has to be in demand, easy to make, and protected from copying.

1826 The first photograph (of roofs and chimneys), is taken by Joseph Niépce of France.

1829 The first train, Stephenson's *Rocket*, speeds along at a record-smashing 30 mph (48 kph).

1876 The box telephone is invented by Alexander Graham Bell. His first words were to his assistant: "Mr. Watson, come here."

1878 Thomas Swan invented the glass bulb and Thomas Edison invented a long-lasting filament.

TECH TIMES

Breakthroughs in technology lead to a burst of inventions. Smaller and cheaper gadgets appear. The power of a roomful of the first computers can fit inside a cell phone.

> Ralph H. Baer is my hero. He invented video gaming in 1967 with the first console.

1962 Spacewar, one of the first computer games, featured two spaceships battling each other.

1965 The first touchscreen device was a tablet made by British engineer E. A. Johnson. It was used by air traffic controllers until 1995.

People are inventing robots with artificial intelligence.

Soon, robots may be smarter than people!

MEGA INVENTIONS

Some inventions are so important that they lead to countless other inventions. The wheel, for example, is used in everything from cars and airplanes to computer hard drives.

We launched the Hubble telescope into space in 1990.

1088 Shen Kuo, a Chinese scientist (1031–1095) discovered that the Earth acts like a huge magnet. He invented the magnetic compass.

1455 Invention of the moveable type printing press.

1608 The telescope helped people look closer at the celestial bodies in the sky.

1783 The French Montgolfier brothers launch the first hot-air balloon capable of carrying people. The balloon flies over Paris for 25 minutes.

In 1895, German Wilhelm Röntgen made a winning invention: X-rays. He won the first Nobel Prize in physics.

1885 The first car, a three-wheeler with no roof that chugged along at 8 mph (13 kph) built by German Karl Benz.

1895 The Lumière brothers patented the cinematograph. Modern cinemas were born.

1903 The *Wright Flyer*, the first airplane. On its maiden voyage it rose 120 feet (37 m) and flew for 12 seconds.

1926 The televison was invented by John Logie Baird of Scotland. In 1953 the first color TV show aired in the US, and in 1988 flatscreen televisions first appeared.

1973 Motorola produced the first handheld mobile phone. It worked for 30 minutes and took 10 hours to recharge.

1977 The Apple 2, a user-friendly personal computer, was invented by Stephen Wozniak and Steve Jobs.

1983 A number of tech innovations lead to the development of the modern Internet. Tim Berners-Lee invented the World Wide Web.

2000 Bill Gates launched Microsoft's touch-input tablet computer. Apple popularized tablets in 2010 with the launch of the iPad.

2004 Mark Zuckerberg created a website to allow friends to connect, which became Facebook.

2005 Video-sharing website YouTube launched to allow users to upload, view, comment on, and rate video content.

ROBOTS

They're here now. In the future, they'll be everywhere: an army of robots in our homes, at our schools, even inside our bodies. Bots are getting busier and brainier. The latest robots are even thinking for themselves.

I'm not here to replace you . . . I'm just here for the par-tay. 24/7!

JOBS FOR THE ROBOTS

Need someone to answer the phone in ten different languages? Or switch on the TV and pass you the remote? ASIMO is the ultimate home helper. Someday robots may take over all our jobs, but for now we can work side by side. Thanks, buddy!

I stay safe while the bot does all the dangerous stuff.

BOT, DO YOU COPY?

FLYING SKY HIGH

One day, our skies will be filled with busy bots. Flying robots can already:

Look for underwater mines
Inspect tall bridges and buildings
Check weather from high up in the sky
Herd sheep from a hillside to their home
Wear robot bee disguises to pollinate plants
Find evidence of lost, buried ancient cities
Film big sporting events from the air
Carry medicines to disaster areas
Deliver mail—and even pizza!

Someday our bodies may be crawling with tiny nanobots, keeping us fit and healthy from the inside. Creepy!

🔵 BUILD IT!   **DESIGN YOUR OWN ROBOT TO EXPLORE THE**

10 things real robots can really do

1. CLEAN WINDOWS 2. WRITE COOKBOOKS 3. PLAY CARDS
4. PRACTICE PING-PONG 5. BE LIFEGUARDS 6. DRIVE CARS AND
TRUCKS 7. PLAY THE PIANO 8. DELIVER ROOM SERVICE
9. COMPETE ON TV GAME SHOWS 10. ZIP UP ZIPPERS
. . . AND ALL WITHOUT A BATHROOM BREAK.

Blinking building bots! I can't control them. They're after my job . . . They're after me!

To keep all those bots from crashing into planes, a new air-traffic-control system will be built.

Hmmm . . . that's no criminal. It's a sheep. Could be a baa-d one, though.

A car-sized roving robot named *Curiosity* makes tracks across Mars, finding out about the planet's history.

Humanoid teacher bot NAO can ask questions and understand answers. NAO is able to help people with autism to learn.

The Atlas robot is being developed to walk rough ground, drill through rocks, and climb using arms and legs, to help rescue people.

OCEANS, FLY THROUGH SPACE, OR EVEN HELP CLEAN YOUR ROOM!

MINI PICS

Hey, a button! I wonder what this does.

click

Whirr . . . clunk. I've been powered up!

Robots need power to move . . .

. . . and sensors and smarts to run!

Raging robot! What do I do?

Give me that. I want to be my own boss!

In the future, robots will power and move themselves—they'll just keep going!

Power-assisted suits will gve you superhuman strength!

You'll be able to *roll* up your **TABLET** like a mat.

Artificial intelligence will make computers that you can talk to just like humans.

TEMPERATURE-CONTROLLED MUGS WILL MAKE SURE YOUR HOT CHOCOLATE IS NOT *TOO* HOT.

Refrigerator

milk   fish

eggs   fruit

meat   cheese

SMART FRIDGES will have screens for looking up recipes. You'll also be able to see inside your fridge using your phone!

We, robots will become workers and even your friends!

98-INCH (2.5 M) TELEVISIONS WITH A PICTURE **SO SHARP** THAT NO PIXELS ARE VISIBLE **AT ALL**.

Fact Attack

A HIGH -TECH FUTURE

The future's coming and it's going to be techtastic. So sit back and switch on!

PLAYER 1

Watch movies with my eyes closed? Seeing is believing!

SOLAR-POWERED PLANES could bring clean energy to air transport.

Send an avatar to school

ACTIVE CONTACT LENSES WILL BECOME MINICOMPUTERS THAT LET YOU WATCH MOVIES AND READ MESSAGES.

Now I'll never put a foot wrong!

Look forward to trainers with self-tightening laces made with foot-scanning technology.

DRIVERLESS CARS WILL COME TO PICK YOU UP, WITH THE PRESS OF A BUTTON ON YOUR PHONE.

DRIVE START STOP

CLOTHES WILL DO EVERYTHING THE SMARTPHONE DOES NOW.

SPACE TOURISM WILL LIFT OFF. CHECK IN FOR A FIVE-NIGHT STAY IN AN ORBITING HOTEL SUITE.

Space begins 50 miles (80 km) above Earth.

Forget going to the shops to buy a new toothbrush, you'll be able to print one on a 3-D printer! Phones, jewelry and even food may be printed for us one day.

VIDEO GAMING GOES AR (AUGMENTED REALITY)—NO DEVICE, AND PLAYING A GAME FEELS LIKE YOU'RE IN THE GAMING REALM.

A SCANDINAVIAN COMPANY IS WORKING ON A WAY **TO TRANSLATE WHAT A DOG IS THINKING.**

OH, NO! I'll be out of a job!

. . . Visit Venice from your sofa . . .

HOVERBOARDS that *really* hover, animated pets, and toys that talk back are all being developed.

Zero-carbon, **sustainable cities**, like Masdar near Abu Dhabi, are under construction now.

GET READY FOR **CRASH-PROOF CARS** USING RADAR, SONAR, AND DRIVER-ALERT SYSTEMS.

Even I, an Alien Villainess, did not know all the facts on page 120. My fact-zapper must be broken. Hand yours over.

Yes, boss.

We are marching to Mars. Meet you there, on page 124.

3,2,1,

Is space the place you'd love to explore? Zoom into an outer-space adventure with the LEGO® minifigures! There's a

Find out what
it's like to be an astronaut
on page 122. Come
spacewalking with me!

We really did make
it to the Moon . . . and
back! Get the facts
on page 118.

I wonder if there
is intelligent life
on Earth?

We're finding
lots of new planets!
See some bad ones
on page 126.

BLAST OFF!

whole galaxy of facts to uncover. Visit the planets and meet
the men, women, and machines exploring the universe.
Turn the page, and let's lift off!

MOON LANDING

There is no air, weather, or life of any kind on the Moon—so why go? Because getting there and surviving on its surface was the greatest human challenge of all time. Let's join moonwalkers Neil Armstrong and Buzz Aldrin on that historic first trip.

When is the Moon not hungry? When it's full.

TRIP TO THE MOON

In 1969, three US astronauts left Earth on a mission called Apollo 11. They were launched by Saturn V, a powerful rocket. When the Apollo 11 crew reached the Moon, a lunar landing module named Eagle dropped down to the surface. Astronauts Neil Armstrong and Buzz Aldrin were the first people to set foot on the Moon. They collected soil samples and left a flag.

Armstrong said that setting foot on the Moon was "one small step for [a] man, one giant leap for mankind."

Apollo 11 launching

Did you know that only 12 people have ever walked on the Moon?

And none since 1972! I wasn't even a mini minifigure, then.

Someday robots will run a space lab on the Moon. Look, there it is!

MINI PICS

10 things left on the Moon by astronauts of past missions

1. BAGS OF PEE 2. EMPTY PACKETS OF SPACE FOOD 3. BLANKETS 4. A HAMMER
5. A PAIR OF BOOTS 6. BACKPACKS 7. USED WET WIPES 8. BLANKETS 9. A RAKE
10. TWO GOLF BALLS (HIT IN 1971 BY APOLLO 14'S ALAN SHEPARD WITH A CLUB HE
HAD SMUGGLED INTO SPACE)

A VIEW TO REMEMBER

The crew members of Apollo 8 were the first to see an "Earthrise," when they flew around the Moon in 1968.

Aldrin and Armstrong explored the Moon's surface for more than two hours.

Three spacesuits were designed for each astronaut—one for training, one for flight, and one for space.

The astronauts collected soil samples and planted an American flag.

With no wind or weather to disturb them, these footprints will remain for millions of years.

IT'S MOON-TASTIC!

The Moon is not round —it's egg-shaped.

The Moon has no atmosphere, so the sky appears black.

Humans may walk on the Moon again. There have been plans to build a base there, to use as a stepping stone to reach Mars.

The Moon doesn't shine. It reflects light from the Sun.

During the day, the temperature on the Moon can reach 253°F (123°C). At night, it can drop to a chilly −387°F (−233°C).

It takes three days to fly to the Moon from Earth.

Earth travels around the Sun at **67,000** miles per hour (108,000 kph). Hold on tight!

1 MILLION Earths could fit inside our Sun.

THERE ARE **2** GOLF BALLS ON THE MOON.

MORE THAN **95 PERCENT** OF THE UNIVERSE IS INVISIBLE TO US.

THERE ARE ABOUT 3 SEPTILLION STARS. THAT'S **3,000,000,000,000, 000,000,000,000.** GIVE OR TAKE 1 OR 2.

If you stood on Mercury, the Sun would look **2 and a half** times bigger than it does on Earth.

Astronaut means "star sailor" . . . cool!

Fact Attack

OUT-THERE NUMBERS IN SPACE

Attention, humans! Prepare your squishy brains to absorb some mind-boggling facts. Read on!

Volcanoes on Mars are **100** times bigger than those on Earth.

The black hole

A single asteroid can contain more gold than has ever been mined on Earth. Mine, all mine!

There are about **half a million** pieces of space junk orbiting Earth. Heads up!

It would take **800** years to fly a jet plane to Pluto.

We are **92,900,000** miles (149,500,000 km) from the Sun. But don't forget to wear sunscreen.

THE SUN ACCOUNTS FOR **99.8 PERCENT** OF THE MASS OF OUR SOLAR SYSTEM.

ERIS, THE COLDEST, FARTHEST OBJECT IN THE SOLAR SYSTEM, TAKES **557** YEARS TO ORBIT EARTH. SLOWPOKE.

THERE ARE **6** AMERICAN FLAGS ON THE MOON.

A full NASA space suit costs **$12 million**.

JUPITER HAS **67** MOONS.

IT WOULD TAKE **130** DAYS TO DRIVE A CAR TO THE MOON.

A single day on Mercury equals **176** days on Earth. Now that *is* upside down.

closest to Earth is about **10,000** light-years away.

THE AVERAGE DISTANCE BETWEEN STARS IS **20 TRILLION** MILES (32 TRILLION KM).

The Moon is moving about **1.5** inches (3.8 cm) away from our planet every year. See you later!

The smallest stars found are 12 miles (19 km) wide.

SPACE STATION

The International Space Station (ISS) is a science lab orbiting Earth, about 220 miles (354 km) above our planet. It completes an orbit every 90 minutes. Look up, you might just see it!

Want to know what it's like to build the ISS? Try building one with LEGO® bricks—but put gloves on first!

Astronauts have to be sick in a "barf bag" or the chunks will float away. Yuck!

THE ISS PIECE BY PIECE

The ISS is about the size of a soccer field. For more than 15 years, separate pieces have been blasted up inside rockets to be fixed on by astronauts. Imagine trying to build while floating in a spacesuit! One astronaut dropped her tool bag in November 2008. It's been orbiting Earth ever since.

SUIT FOR SPACE

When the ISS needs an outside repair, it's time for a spacewalk. A spacesuit has everything an astronaut needs: oxygen, carbon dioxide removal, and pressure controls. Fourteen layers protect the astronaut from scorching-hot sunshine or freezing shade. The longest space walk was 8 hours and 56 minutes.

LIVING IN SPACE

Astronauts regularly stay on the ISS for about six months. Samantha Cristoforetti stayed for 199 days at one time, the longest stay of a female astronaut, leaving in June 2015.

6 weird things to get used to on the ISS

1. NO SHOWERS—SPONGE BATHS ONLY 2. FOOD AND DRINKS STORED IN POUCHES (TO STOP THEM FROM FLOATING AWAY) 3. NO SALT OR PEPPER— THE SPRINKLES FLOAT INTO THE INSTRUMENTS, CAUSING DAMAGE 4. A TOILET LIKE A VACUUM CLEANER 5. NO BED—JUST A SLEEPING BAG FASTENED TO A WALL 6. TWO-HOUR DAILY EXERCISE SESSIONS TO STOP YOUR MUSCLES TURNING TO JELLY

packet of space food

ESSENTIAL DELIVERIES

About four times a year, food and equipment are delivered to the ISS by unmanned spacecraft. After they've taken away waste, some of these spacecraft burn up in Earth's atmosphere.

THINGS TO DO ON THE ISS

Play soccer, upside down!

Chase balls of juice around the pod and catch them with your mouth.

Cry the biggest tear! Tears do not float away on the ISS—they collect in a huge water bubble on your face.

Spot countries on Earth from the viewing pod.

Go for a (space) walk— although it takes 8 to 12 hours to prepare for one!

MINI PICS

Yawn! I need a good night's sleep. Ready, Teddy?

Sleeping's a little different up here, with no up or down. Climb into your crew cabin. You don't want to float around and bump into things, so attach your sleeping bag to the wall.

Teddy, I'm attaching YOU to me. Big squeeze!

123

THE RED PLANET

It's super stormy, super dusty, and there's very little oxygen. But don't worry about all that! Plans are afoot to land the first humans on Mars. Are you tough enough to take a trip to the red planet? Better read this quick guide first.

It would take 271 years and 221 days to get to Mars by car. Mars is far out, dude!

WHERE IS MARS?

Mars is the fourth planet from our Sun, at a distance of 141.71 million miles (228.1 km). It's atmosphere is too thin to keep in heat. So Mars is freezing cold, with an average temperature of about −82°F (−63°C).

Earth   Mars

WATER ON MARS

In September 2015, new findings from NASA's Mars Reconnaisance Orbiter revealed the strongest evidence yet that liquid water may sometimes flow on Mars. Researchers saw minerals in mysterious streaks. The streaks seem to move over time as though they flow, when temperatures are above −10°F (−23°C). These flows may be related to liquid water.

MINI PICS

Streaks of water on Mars? Send me to explore!

Hold on a sec. You might have germs from Earth.

I was just curious.

● BUILD IT!   BUILD A ROVER TO SNOOP AROUND A PLANET. MAKE SURE IT CAN

1. CLIMB OLYMPUS MONS, A VOLCANO THREE TIMES HIGHER THAN EVEREST 2. TAKE A DESERT HIKE 3. EXPLORE SOME CAVES 4. TREK THROUGH THE SOLAR SYSTEM'S LARGEST CANYON, VALLES MARINERIS, 5 MILES (8 KM) DEEP 5. ICE-SKATE AT THE POLES 6. CHECK OUT ONE OF 43,000 LARGE CRATERS, CREATED BY ASTEROID IMPACTS

CURIOSITY ROVER

In 2012, a rocket-powered flying crane lowered space rover *Curiosity* onto the surface of Mars. Since then, it's been trundling around at a speed of 2 in (5 cm) per second, taking photos and testing samples of rock and soil. It's trying to figure out if there was water and life billions of years ago.

HUMANS ON MARS

NASA is hoping to send the first astronauts to Mars in the 2030s. When they arrive, they will build a shelter to protect themselves from the cold and the solar radiation. The astronauts will also have to construct a power source to produce oxygen for breathing and growing food.

Why do those crazy Earthlings want to go to Mars? It's way too chilly!

EXOPLANETS

YOU WOULD NO WAY WANT TO LIVE ON . . .

1. Too easy to get lost on—Kepler-10c is 2.3 times bigger than Earth.

2. Too bad for the hair—GJ1214b is very hot and wet. Even the air is mostly water.

3. Too speedy—COROT-Exo-7b whizzes around its sun in just 20 hours. And it's scorching hot.

4. Too chilly—OGLE-2005-BLG-390Lb is the coldest planet ever discovered. Its surface temperature is about −370°F (−223°C).

5. Too fiery—Kepler-70b is a scorcher because it's super close to its sun. Its surface temperature is a sizzling 12,398°F (−6,870°C).

6. Too deadly—COROT-7b rains rocks down onto oceans of lava. Ouch! There's nowhere to hide!

7. Too freaky—TrES-2b is close to its sun, but mega-dark. It's so dark, it reflects less light than coal or matte black paint.

8. Too confusing—Fomalhaut B zigzags its way around its sun, sometimes 4.5 billion miles (7.2 billion km) from it, sometimes 27 billion miles (43.5 billion km).

9. Too bling—55 Cancri e is thought to be made completely of diamonds. And it's eight times bigger than Earth!

An exoplanet orbits a star that isn't our Sun.

Let's check out the powder on the nearest exoplanet! How long to get there?

12 years if you travel at the speed of light. It's 70 trillion miles (113 trillion km) away.

Yawn . . . Wake me up when we get there.

COOL VEHICLES

Hop on board and zoom across land, sea, and air. Check out the emergency vehicles that save lives, meet mighty machines building big, and chase record-breaking vehicles with a need for speed. Let's go!

BIG MACHINES

Say hello to the mightiest machines on the planet as they cut, lift, push, crush, and dig to build and demolish our town and cities.

Builders' helmets are called hard hats.

MONSTER MACHINES

Want to build big? You'll need BIG machines! Check out these monsters.

DUMP-TRUCK GIANT

These beasts may be more than 20 feet (6 m) high and 50 feet (15 m) long. Each tire is almost twice as tall as a person. There are driverless versions, too!

BORING BRUTE

This monster is better known as the "mole." It grips tunnel walls, then thrusts its huge cutting wheel forward to devour solid rock.

SEA MONSTER

This is not a ship —it's the largest floating crane in the world. *Thialf* is more than 660 feet (201 m) long and has two giant cranes.

SHOVELING BEAST

Giant diggers, more than three stories high, can shift 9,000 tons of soil in one hour. These excavators cost more than $10 million each.

TERRAIN TORMENTOR

Mining excavators are the largest vehicles on Earth. They can be 700 feet (213 m) long with a 70-foot (21 m) bucket-wheel that carves into the ground.

Some crawler cranes can lift 3,000 tons, the weight of 600 elephants!

BUILD IT!

MAKE A TOWERING CRANE. USE STRING TO TIE ON A

INCREDIBLE CRANE

A crawler crane moves easily over bumpy ground on caterpillar tracks, and rotates to swing its long boom into place. A hook on a steel cable attaches to the load. The crane doesn't topple due to heavy counterweights on its base.

WRECKING BALL OR A LIFTING HOOK.

EMERGENCY!

Help! Call 9-1-1! Emergency vehicles whizz trained officers and equipment to the scene. These machines, adapted to save lives, are some of the most interesting vehicles of all.

Let's go! I'll bring officers and equipment. You speed on ahead!

Roger that. My top speed is 130 miles per hour (210 kph).

FIRE-FIGHTING TRUCK

Engines have hoses, water and foam tanks, ladders, cutting tools, medical kits—and a crew of firefighters.

TOUGH TRUCK

A steel, armor-plated police truck with fold-out shields can handle the toughest of emergencies. With four-wheel drive and large rugged wheels, bumpy terrain poses no problem for this mean machine.

TWO-WHEELED WONDER

Nimble in traffic, police motorcycles are perfect for cities. They are fitted with radios, sirens, warning lights, and medical kits. This makes the bikes very heavy, so police drivers are specially trained.

Breathing equipment pro me from sm and gases

DO NOT CROSS

● BUILD IT! **MAKE A RESCUE VEHICLE THAT CAN GO ON LAND AND WATER!**

Check out my yellow floats, or pontoons. They help me land on the sea!

Some fireboats can pump water 400 feet (122 m) into the air.

Don't squirt me! I'm trying to land!

FIREBOAT
In just one minute, some fireboats can suck up 50,000 gallons (189,271 L) of water and pump it at a fire on a ship or in a port.

AIR AMBULANCE
In remote places, special planes transport patients to faraway hospitals. Each year, the 66 planes of Australia's Flying Doctor Service fly the distance of 30 return trips to the Moon to help 100,000 people.

HOVERING HELICOPTER
Police helicopters have searchlights and heat sensors to track criminals by night. Helicopters can take off and land in small awkward places. One even landed on the summit of Mount Everest in 2005!

I'm the Fire Chief. I don't ride in the truck—I have a car that acts as a mobile command unit.

DO NOT CROSS

133

IN THE AIR

Right now, almost one million people are cruising through the skies in planes coordinated by air traffic control. But look up—you might also see a hot-air balloon, a drone, or an ultralight.

The highest skydive began 26 miles (42 km) above Earth!

Good afternoon, this is your pilot speaking. We are cruising at an altitude of 33,000 feet (9,144 m).

Did the pilot just say we're cruising with attitude?

FAST AND HIGH

July 28, 1976, was a busy day for the Lockheed SR-71. One "Blackbird" flew to a record height of 85,069 feet (25,929 m). Another hurtled along at 2,193 miles per hour (3,530 kph), a speed record that still stands today.

London's Heathrow Airport processes 53 million bags each year and has 30 miles (48 km) of conveyor belts.

BUILD IT!

MAKE THE FASTEST FLYING

Altitude! It means height above sea level. *Cruising* is the level part of the flight between ascent and descent.

Check out my *supersonic* jet! Jets that break the speed of sound are used to train astronauts.

My retractable skis help me land in icy Arctic lands.

With a wingspan of about 260 feet (80 m), the double-decker, four-engined Airbus 380 is the largest passenger plane of all time.

A gas burner heats the air inside a colorful billowing "envelope." The hot air is lighter than the surrounding cooler air, so the balloon rises.

SCANNING THE SKY

In a large busy airport, one plane takes off or lands every 45 seconds. Each one is monitored and instructed by air-traffic controllers in a central tower. Radar is used to plot the position of planes.

Like a go-cart with wings, a motorized ultralight can weigh as little as 250 pounds (113 kg), less than two people.

Need a bird's-eye view to assess a forest fire or search a remote desert? Send in a drone, an unpiloted computer-controlled aircraft.

The longest runway in the world is in China. It stretches for 3.4 miles (5.5 km). The shortest, on Caribbean island Saba, is 0.25 miles (0.4 km).

Becoming a rescue swimmer in the US Coast Guard is extremely tough. Only around 900 people have ever passed the training.

SEARCH AND RESCUE

Air-sea rescues can involve coordinating helicopters, seaplanes, and boats. The mission is simple: to get people out of the water before they come to any major harm. Helicopters fly in to lower winchmen or rescue swimmers into the ocean or onto the deck of a stranded vessel. This team is practicing a rescue with a training dummy. Helicopters and their crews are also especially helpful in mountain rescues.

FIVE RECORD-BREAKING SPEED CHAMPIONS!

Helmets on, fasten your seat belts! We're off on a hair-raising ride with some of the greatest speed champs of all time. In specially built vehicles powered by rockets, jets, or simply leg muscles, these daring drivers zoomed to new world records.

ROCKET PLANE PILOT

Faster even than the jet-engined Blackbird (see page 134) is the rocket-powered North American X-15. It has held the world speed record for a rocket-plane since 1967, when Major William J. Knight flew at 4,520 miles per hour (7,274 kph). The X-15 soared so close to the edge of space that its pilots were given astronaut badges.

SUPERSONIC DRIVER

In 1997 in Black Rock Desert, Nevada, British driver Andy Green's car, *Thrust SSC*, became the first car to break the speed of sound. It hit 763 miles per hour (1,228 kph), the fastest speed ever achieved by a land vehicle.

MOTORBIKE MASTER

The fastest person on two wheels is US motorcycle rider Rocky Robinson. In 2010, his streamlined Ack Attack bike zoomed to an incredible 394 miles per hour (634 kph).

WATER WHIZ

Australian Ken Warby holds the world water speed record. He built a "hydroplane" (water plane) in his own backyard, using wood, fiberglass, and a cheap jet engine. In 1978, his boat, *Spirit of Australia*, powered across a lake, reaching 318 miles per hour (511 kph).

PEDAL POWERHOUSE

Barbara Buatois from France might say that using an engine is cheating. In 2010, she pedaled her streamlined recumbent bicycle to a cracking 76 miles per hour (122 kph)—the fastest speed ever in a vehicle powered by a woman.

VARNA-24

In a Formula 1 race, about 20 open-wheeled, single-seat cars zoom around the track. It's too dangerous to attempt speed records.

The Italian circuit at Monza is the fastest track.

Octan

5

ON THE OCEAN

Today, there are boats adapted for every need— huge supertankers piled high with containers, fishing vessels loaded with nets, light watercraft for police crews, submarines for underwater adventures, and powerboats built purely for speed.

> Slow down, speedy!

> But I'm on a powerboat! I can hit 200 miles per hour (322 kph)!

SUPERTANKER

Steel ocean giants, more than 1,300 feet (396 m) long and 197 feet (60 m) wide, transport huge containers of goods all over the world.

FISHING VESSEL

Almost 100 million tons of fish are caught each year. Fishing boats have powerful winches to lift the heavy nets.

POWERFUL POWERBOAT

Powerboats are long and thin—this streamlining helps them cut through the water quickly. Cockpits are reinforced with roll bars to prevent them collapsing if the boats flip.

> About 3 million shipwrecks lie on the ocean floor. Perfect for treasure-hunting! Oo-arr!

BUILD IT!

MAKE A CRUISE SHIP LIKE A FLOATING CITY.

3 fascinating things washed up on beaches

1. 28,000 RUBBER DUCKS FELL OFF A SHIP IN 1992 AND THEIR JOURNEYS—FROM AUSTRALIA TO ALASKA—PROVIDE DATA ABOUT OCEAN CURRENTS 2. GIANT EYEBALL, THE SIZE OF A SOFTBALL, BELONGING TO A SWORDFISH 3. PART OF A SPACE ROCKET

WATER PATROL

Police use inflatable boats—they are light and easy to transport. Gas-filled tubes keep them afloat if they take on too much water.

ANCHORS AWEIGH!

The world's largest anchor belonged to supertanker *Seawise Giant*. It weighed a colossal 36 tons and was 23 feet (7 meters) long.

ARCTIC ICEBREAKER

With strong, shaped hulls and underwater air jets, icebreakers can cut through thick ice, moving forward or backward.

STEEL SUBMARINE

Every submarine has its own "crush depth," which can be up to 2,400 feet (732 m). If the sub dives to its crush depth, the water pressure will squash it like a tin can.

THE LONGEST AND HEAVIEST AIRPLANE IS THE AN-225 *MRIYA*. THIS CARGO PLANE IS 275 FEET (84 M) LONG AND WEIGHS 314 TONS.

THE FASTEST ROAD CAR YOU CAN BUY IS THE **HENNESSEY VENOM GT**. IT TRAVELS AT 270.49 MPH (435 KPH).

In 2002, Steve Fossett took just over 14 days to **fly nonstop around the world** in a hot-air balloon.

The longest train ever had 682 wagons, 8 locomotives, and was 4.5 miles (7.3 km) long!

The FASTEST SPEED on an unaltered **lawn mower** is 61 mph (98 kph)!

Woo-hoo, life in the fast lane!

Fact Attack

The biggest privately owned superyacht is 728 feet (222 m) long. It cost more than one billion dollars to build!

THINGS *THAT GO!*

Check out the fastest, biggest, longest . . . trains, planes, probes, cars, and even lawn mowers!

There are an estimated

KEVIN FAST pulled a 126,200-pound (57,243 kg) fire truck 100 feet (30 m) to break the world record.

Kevin has also pulled a house and a plane. Strong!

The most expensive car in the world is the **Lamborghini Veneno Roadster**. It costs $4.5 million.

There are at least 5,000 commercial airplanes flying over the United States at any one time.

THE FASTEST-MOVING VEHICLES EVER WERE THE HELIOS SPACE PROBES THAT REACHED 157,000 MPH (252,000 KPH) AS THEY RACED AROUND THE SUN.

The LEGO Group is the world's biggest tire manufacturer. It makes **318 million tiny tires** every year!

The largest LEGO® wheel is 4.2 inches (10.7 cm) high and belongs to the Power Puller car.

It would take 500 days to cycle to the Moon—if you went 20 mph (32 kph) without a break.

MORE THAN **21.5 MILLION VW BEETLES** HAVE BEEN SOLD. IT'S ONE OF THE BEST-SELLING CARS OF ALL TIME.

TO SHOW THEIR SIZE AND SHAPE IN THE DARK, SOME LARGE TRUCKS ARE COVERED IN MORE THAN 100 LIGHTS.

1 billion bikes in the world— double the amount of cars.

60110

A CALIFORNIA TOWN IS FAMED FOR ITS COLLECTION OF MORE THAN 80,000 HUBCAPS!

THE LONGEST ROAD SUITABLE FOR CARS IS **THE PAN-AMERICAN HIGHWAY.** IT BEGINS IN ALASKA AND ENDS IN ARGENTINA.

143

Check out five of the greatest moments in sports history on page 148.

When I see snow, I say, Go! Get with the winter sports on page 150.

Surf's up on page 152. Phew, what a wave!

SPORTS CRAZY

Are you a football fanatic, a surfer dude, a record-breaking champion, or a mighty Olympian? Or just an all-around good sport? The LEGO® minifigures are here to get sporty. They race, they leap, they throw, they score! The crowd goes crazy!

145

THE OLYMPICS

From gymnastics to wrestling, swimming to wheelchair tennis, there's an Olympic sport for everyone. So join in the fun at the biggest sporting event on the planet. There are medals and glory to be won.

One ancient wrestler trained by carrying a calf every day. As the calf grew, he got stronger.

ANCIENT OLYMPICS

The first Olympics were held in 776 BCE in Greece. The games took place for four days in the city of Olympia.

Olympic Stadium, Beijing, China

FASTER, HIGHER, STRONGER
(CITIUS, ALTIUS, FORTIUS)

This is the motto of the modern Olympic Games, which began in 1894. The Olympic games has been held every four years since (it has only been canceled in three years). The Paralympics began in England in 1948 and is always held in the weeks following the Olympics.

In 490 BCE, Pheidippides, a Greek soldier, ran 26 miles (42 km) to pass a message from Marathon to Athens. The first marathon!

USA has won a men's wheelchair basketball gold medal a record SEVEN times!

The first female Olympic champion was Charlotte Cooper in 1900. She played in a full, ankle-length dress!

14 Olympic events that really did exist . . .

1. POODLE CLIPPING 2. PLUNGING 3. SWIMMING OBSTACLE RACE
4. CROQUET 5. TUG-OF-WAR 6. SOLO SYNCHRONIZED SWIMMING
7. ROLLER HOCKEY 8. EQUESTRIAN LONG JUMP 9. ROPE CLIMBING
10. TANDEM BICYCLE 2000-METER SPRINT 11. ONE-HANDED
WEIGHTLIFTING 12. UNDERWATER SWIMMING 13. STANDING
HIGH JUMP 14. POLO

BUILD IT! **BUILD AN OLYMPIC TRACK FOR YOUR CHAMPION ATHLETES.**

The five Olympic rings represent the union of five continents.

The five continents are: Africa, the Americas, Asia, Australia, and Europe.

The continent of Antarctica is not represented because nobody is resident there.

Every country in the Olympics has at least one of the ring colors in their flag.

The symbol was designed by Pierre de Coubertin, a founder of the modern Olympics.

In 1900, in France, winners won paintings instead of medals.

The first ever Olympic team game was soccer. Kick, pass, goal!

The Olympic torch is lit in Greece and travels to the country hosting the games.

Most Olympic Games take out, or introduce new games. Judo and taekwondo are Olympic sports. But karate got the chop!

FACTASTIC FIVE

FIVE GREAT SPORTING MOMENTS

I t's the moment sporting fans sometimes wait all their lives to see. The rare moment, when an individual or a whole team perform a sporting act so awesome that it goes down in history.

1982 NATIONAL FOOTBALL LEAGUE, "THE CATCH"

The Dallas Cowboys have dominated the NFL since 1970. There are 51 seconds of an NFC Championship game left, when Dwight Clark, of the San Francisco 49ers, makes a spectacular catch that sets up an extra kick point that leads them to a 28–27 victory. It is the end of the Cowboys' rule.

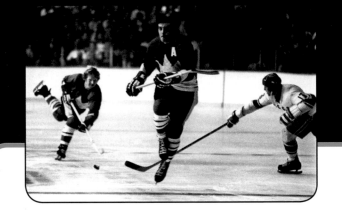

1972 CANADA V. SOVIET UNION

An eight-game showdown between the two superpowers of ice hockey. The Soviets are in the lead after the first five games. Then in a spectacular turnaround, Canada go onto win the last three games in Moscow. A last-minute goal by Paul Henderson gives the Canadians a 6–5 victory in the final game. Canada wins the series.

1986 WORLD CUP QUARTER FINAL "GOAL OF THE CENTURY"

Argentinian Diego Maradona deftly dribbles the ball past five England players and finally shoots it past the goalkeper to score. England are devastated. Argentina wins 2–1, and goes on to win the World Cup.

148

2001 US OPEN, SISTERS MEET

It's the final of the 2001 US Open, between two sisters, Venus and Serena Williams. The game lasts 69 minutes. At one point, Venus smashes a 109 mph (175 kph) serve that knocks the racket from Serena's hand. Venus wins 6-2, 6-4 in a bittersweet victory.

2004 RED SOX COMEBACK

Picture this: The Boston Red Sox trail the New York Yankees, three games to none in the American League Championship Series. Then, in an unprecedented success, they win the next four games to knock out the Yankees, their big rivals. The Red Sox go on to win the World Series.

The longest tennis Grand Slam final? The 2012 Australian Open men's singles final. Novak Djokovic defeated Rafael Nadal after FIVE hours, FIFTY-THREE minutes.

Ha! The longest professional baseball game lasted for 33 innings, with EIGHT hours and TWENTY-FIVE minutes.

WINTER OLYMPICS

Brace yourselves, it's the Winter Olympics! It's all about snow, ice, and some incredible speeds. The first Winter Games was held in 1924, in France. The original five sports were bobsleigh, curling, ice hockey, Nordic skiing, and skating. In 2018, the Winter Olympics will be in Pyeong Chang, South Korea.

Norway has won the most medals in Winter Olympic history.

RECORD TORCH JOURNEY

The 2014 Sochi Games torch traveled on an epic trip including the North Pole, the bottom of the world's deepest lake, and even into space, to the International Space Station.

SPEEDSTERS

For those who want speed lying down, look no further than the luge. Manuel Pfister of Austria, shot down a track at a top speed of 95.69 mph (154 kph)!

Ski jumpers launch from hills up to 394 feet (120 m) high. A jumper can remain in the air for 7 seconds. That's flying!

The youngest individual gold medallist was American figure skater Tara Lipinski, aged 15 at the 1998 Games in Japan.

211

8 FASTEST WINTER SPORTS EVER!

1. SNOWBOARDING, 125 MPH (201 KPH) 2. DOWNHILL SKIING, 100.6 MPH (161.9 KPH) 3. LUGE, 95.69 MPH (154 KPH) 4. BOBSLED, 95.1 MPH (153 KPH) 5. SKELETON, 87.5 MPH (140.8 KPH) 6. SKI JUMP, 59.7 MPH (96.1 KPH) 7. SPEED SKATING 36.8 MPH (59.2 KPH) 8. THE GOLD MEDAL FOR THE FASTEST OBJECT GOES TO . . . THE PUCK IN ICE HOCKEY, 110.3 MPH (177.5 KPH)

SNOW CHAMP

Norwegian cross-country skier Bjørn Dæhlie is the Winter medal champ. He has won 8 golds and 4 silver medals in three Olympics.

Snowboarding was introduced to the Winter Olympics in 1998. Norwegian Torstein Horgmo was the first to perform a triple cork—three flicks. Awesome!

American Eddie Eagan is the only person to have won a gold medal at both the Winter and Summer Olympics! For the four-man bobsled team and boxing.

Ice hockey and figure skating were originally part of the Summer Olympics.

Curling was invented in Scotland. All the stones used in curling are made in Scotland or Wales. Better keep hold of my brush!

Officially the largest wave ever surfed was 78 feet (23.7 m) by American Garrett McNamara, 2001, off the Portugese coast.

SURF'S UP!

Ever since Polynesian Islanders, over 3,000 years ago, picked up a wooden board and "rode" the waves, the quest to find the perfect wave has persisted. Every wave is different, and surfers learn to use their skills to keep riding them. Modern surfing is not just a sport but has become an entire culture, with cool words and fashion style.

UNUSUAL SPORTS
RECORD BREAKERS

1. To make the world's largest ever vertical skydiving formation, 164 skydivers created this giant flower in the sky over Chicago in July 2015.

2. American Darren Taylor dived 33 ft 10 in (10.3 m) into a pool of water 12 in (30 cm) deep to win the world shallow dive record.

3. Dan Magness, from the UK, kept a soccer ball up for 26 hours using just his feet, legs, shoulders, and head.

4. Christopher Irmscher, from Germany, ran the 100-meter hurdles in 14.82 seconds, wearing flippers!

5. Thaneswar Guragai, from Nepal, bounced a basketball 444 times in one minute.

6. In 2013, Japan's Kenichi Ito completed the fastest 100-meter run ON ALL FOURS in 16.87 seconds.

7. In 2006, American Daniel Smith, (nicknamed The Rubber Boy) passed his body through a tennis racket 3 times in one minute!

8. The fastest skateboard speed from a standing start is 80.74 mph (129.94 kph), set by Mischo Erban in 2012.

9. In 2013, Krystian Herba, from Poland, climbed all 2,754 steps of the World Financial Center in Shanghai, China on a bike! It took 1 hour, 21 minutes.

10. In Australia, in 2012, 145 waterskiers were pulled along by one single boat.

I want to break a record.

OK, why not try to drive a golf ball the farthest ever? Go, Grandma, Go, Grandma!

I'd like to see you try! No one has beaten Mike Austin's record of 1,545 ft (470.9 m) since 1974!

Actually, astronaut Alan Shepard hit a golf ball off the Moon. No one knows how far that went!

I'll bet no one has tried hitting a golf ball while surfing a wave. I'll be famous!

Check out the crazy constructions made of LEGO® bricks on page 160!

It's a song and dance on stage on page 166. Curtain up, please!

Rock with us through musical history on page 159!

FUN

From ballet, buildings, and books to all things musical, this section is your

STUFF

ticket to a world of culture. Open your eyes to a world of entertainment, be stunned by awe-inspiring buildings, and above all, enjoy!

FIVE
FAVORITE SOUNDS OF MUSIC

Whether you like jazz or classical, disco or rap, or just jamming to a little rock, there is a sound for everyone out there. All music has roots that can be traced back hundreds or thousands of years, but every once in a while a new sound emerges and takes the world by storm.

LET'S ROCK!

Rock music developed out of "Rock and Roll" during the 1960s. Rock bands are known for their BIG sounds. British band, Led Zeppelin, once reached 130 decibels during a particularly loud concert!
THAT'S LOUD.

ALL THAT JAZZ

Jazz was born in New Orleans about 100 years ago, but its roots can be found in the musical traditions of both Africa and Europe. The world's largest jazz festival is the Festival International de Jazz de Montréal in Quebec, Canada. 3,000 artists perform 650 concerts, which attract over 2 million jazz visitors!

POP STARS

Pop songs are short, basic tunes that repeat choruses, melodic tunes, and hooks. The "Queen of Pop" is Madonna. She is the most successful female musician of all time. She has also acted in more than 20 films. She's a busy pop star!

RAP ARTISTS

Rapping has its roots in old African storytelling from centuries ago. It has rhythmic lyrics that accompany hip hop music. The first rappers to win the Best Rap Performance Grammy were DJ Jazzy Jeff & The Fresh Prince (aka Will Smith) in 1988, with "Parents Just Don't Understand."

CLASSICAL MUSIC

Most classical music is written for orchestras that may have up to 90 instruments led by a conductor. The largest ever orchestra consisted of a whopping 7,224 musicians, in 2013, in Australia! They played Queen's "We Will Rock You" among other pieces.

AMAZING BUILDINGS

Some buildings invite us to slow down, look around, and take in the view. They say a lot about the people who built them, the story of the times they lived in, and what they wanted to leave for the future. They inpsire us to create our own fantastic builds.

The Egyptians were great early architects because of our awesome pyramids.

So no one is actually going to live in that beautiful building?

Eight Boeing 747s could sit wing to wing on the Sydney Opera House site.

As well as building the Eiffel Tower, Gustav Eiffel helped to build the Statue of LIberty.

Sydney Opera House, Sydney, Australia
This was built by Danish architect Jørn Utzon and opened in 1973. The roof is made from huge, interlocking shells.

Taj Mahal, Agra, India
Believed to be one of the most beautiful buildings in the world, this was built by the Mughal emperor Shah Jahan (ruled1628–1658) to house the tomb of his wife.

Eiffel Tower, Paris, France This was built by the engineer Gustave Eiffel in 1889, who said that it celebrated science and industry. It was made up of 18,000 iron pieces.

BUILD IT!   **MAKE THE MOST FANTASTIC BUILDING YOU CAN IMAGINE!**

King Kong, was the giant gorilla who climbed the Empire State Building in the famous film!

4 epic LEGO® brick builds

1. THE KENNEDY SPACE CENTER, USING 750,000 LEGO BRICKS, COVERING 1,506 SQUARE FEET (140 SQ M)
2. A FULL-SIZE BRICK HOUSE WITH A HOT SHOWER AND A BED, USING 3.3 MILLION BRICKS 3. HOGWARTS SCHOOL OF WITCHCRAFT AND WIZARDRY, USING 400,000 BRICKS
4. ALLIANZ ARENA, A STADIUM BUILT FROM 400,000 BRICKS WITH 30,000 MINI FANS INSIDE!

MINI PICS

I'd like a house in the shape of a teapot, with a leaning spout.

I'm afraid I can't do a leaning spout, it's impossible.

There are 6,514 windows in the Empire State Building. Sigh. It's a dirty job!

Hmm, Let's hope repainting isn't an option on this one!

No, it's not. Look at the Leaning Tower of Pisa!

Grandma, the Leaning Tower was a mistake. While they were building it, it started to lean. One day it will fall . . .

It's been leaning for almost 1,000 years! I won't need mine for that long!

Sigh . . .

Empire State Building, New York, US When this building opened on May 1, 1931, it was the tallest building in the world, standing at 1,250 feet (381 m) tall.

St Basil's Cathedral, Moscow, Russia Built in the 16th century by Russian ruler Ivan the Terrible, it has 9 chapels each with a dramatically decorated dome.

Oooh, and I've seen some balconies in the shape of teacups on the Niimi building in Tokyo . . .

161

CRAZY
CONSTRUCTIONS

1. Take a trip to Gettorf, Germany, to check out this upside-down house. All the furniture inside is topsy-turvy, too.

2. The John Hancock Tower in Boston used to sway in the wind, making people feel seasick.

3. Sweden's Ice Hotel melts every summer. It is rebuilt in the winter with 10,000 tons of compacted snow.

4. Architects in Holland are developing the first house made entirely on a 3-D printer.

5. A treehouse made from an airplane nestles in a Costa Rican jungle as part of a luxury hotel.

6. A hotel in Shanghai has a glass-bottomed swimming pool suspended from the 24th floor. Perfect for peering down on the street below.

7. A Bulgarian house is shaped like a snail. It is five stories high, has no straight walls or corners, and is made from eco-friendly materials.

8. In Rotterdam, in the Netherlands, 38 houses that are perfect cubes are situated at different angles so they look like trees in a forest.

9. Selfridges department store in Birmingham, England, is curved, and covered in 15,000 shiny aluminium discs on a blue background.

Every year, there's a race up the 1,576 steps of the Empire State Building. Who's coming?

I'm up for it! Speed is my game!

I'll come, too. I might see myself from the top!

The world's fastest elevator travels at 45 miles per hour (72 kph). Why walk? Yawn.

I have a pizza to deliver to the 86th floor. Let's go!

The tallest LEGO® tower was built by 18,000 builders (many of them children) in Milan, Italy, in 2015.

AMAZING ARCHITECTURE

Want to build something incredible? Look no further than the Nagoya Science Museum in Japan. Inside the ball-shaped dome is the world's biggest planetarium, which is 115 ft (35m) in diameter. The dome is suspended between two 12-story-high "green walls" filled with plants. The best architecture can spark the imagination of young builders like you. Get creative and make an incredible structure. What will you build today?

IN THE THEATER

Theater, as a form of entertainment, developed 2,500 years ago. The ancient Greeks built great amphitheaters to perform specially written funny, sad, or political plays. Over the years, many forms of theater evolved. Let the show go on!

The longest opera is *Die Meistersinger von Nürnberg* by Richard Wagner and lasts 5 hours, 15 minutes! I'll bring my teddy!

In an opera, all the words are sung. Wolfgang Amadeus Mozart (1756–1791) wrote 22 operas!

Swan Lake is considered the most popular ballet of all time. Oh, to be a swan!

Cats is one of the longest-running musicals of all time. Purrr-fect!

"Break a leg" means good luck in theater. If I break a leg, I'll be in a cast for months!

Actors are called thespians after Thespis, the first actor.

Mozart wrote his first opera when he was only 12 years old.

Ballet began in Italy in the 16th century, and soon became popular in France.

The first modern musical– *The Black Crook*, was based on a book by Charles M. Barras. It opened in 1866.

The Ancient Greeks had a crane called a mechane, used to help actors "fly" across the stage! Weee!

I'm telling you, that William Shakespeare is going to make a fortune.

TIME LINE

6th century BCE
Greek priest Thespis is known as the first actor and wins the first award. The envelope, please!

2nd century BCE
Comedy plays are a crowd-pleasing part of the Roman games.

500 CE
Most theater disappears in Europe. Religious plays later become popular.

1374
The Japanese say yes to Noh. Classical musical drama that is still regularly performed today.

1550s
Actors travel from town to town in Europe performing plays.

1564
William Shakespeare is born in England.

1576
The first permanent theater is opened in London, UK.

1716
First American theater

1750
First playhouse in New York

1926
Television invented

1943-59
The Golden Age of the Broadway Musical

Kabuki was invented by a woman called Okuni in around 1603.

Clowns today are associated with circuses, but ancient Greeks had clowns, too!

The Lion King is the biggest musical of all time. Tune!

New York City houses the greatest number of theaters, with 420, 40 of which are on Broadway.

Kabuki is a popular form of Japanese theater, with music and amazing costumes and effects.

DISSES
BY WILLIAM SHAKESPEARE

1. Toads, beetles, bats, light on you!

2. Away, you mouldy rogue, away!

3. You scullion! You rampallian! You fustilarian! I'll tickle your catastrophe.

4. Truly, thou art . . . like an ill-roasted egg.

5. You elf-skin, you dried neat's tongue . . . you stock-fish!

6. Is his head worth a hat?

7. He's a most notable coward, an infinite and endless liar, an hourly promise breaker.

8. Pray you, stand further from me.

9. The rascally, scald, beggarly, lousy, pragging knave.

10. I do wish thou wert a dog, that I might love thee something.

11. Thou art a boil, a plague-sore, an embossed carbuncle, in my corrupted blood.

12. Away, you three-inch fool!

13. Methinks thou art a general offense.

14. Eat my leek.

Dumbledore means "bumblebee" in old English. J. K. Rowling chose the name for Harry Potter's headmaster because she pictured him humming to himself.

The money from J. M. Barrie's book *Peter Pan* goes to the Great Ormond Street Hospital for children in London, England.

Teeny Ted from Turnip Town is the world's smallest book. It cost $15,000 to produce and it's so minuscule it fits on a human hair.

THE BESTSELLING SINGLE VOLUME BOOK OF ALL TIME IS *THE LORD OF THE RINGS* (150 MILLION COPIES) BY J. R. R. TOLKIEN.

SIX EDITORS, FIVE DESIGNERS, AND MANY LEGO® MINIFIGURES ALL HELPED TO MAKE THIS BOOK.

Fact Attack

John Steinbeck's original manuscript for *Of Mice and Men* was eaten by a dog.

The first US e-book was a copy of the Declaration of Independence.

READ ALL ABOUT IT

You're reading a book about facts. Well, here are some facts about books.

Reading makes you smarter, keeps you sharp, and makes you a better writer, too.

One copy of *The Little*

C. S. Lewis destroyed the first version of *The Lion, the Witch and the Wardrobe* because his friends criticized it.

Charles Dickens built a tunnel from his main house to a little house where he wrote.

Alice in Wonderland has been translated into 176 languages.

A fairy tale about a runaway gingerbread cookie was first published in 1875. Sweet!

THE **MOST VALUABLE BOOK** IN THE WORLD IS A COPY OF JOHN JAMES AUDUBON'S *BIRDS OF AMERICA*. IT IS WORTH OVER **$10 MILLION**.

DR. SEUSS'S EDITOR CHALLENGED HIM TO WRITE A BOOK USING ONLY 50 WORDS. THE RESULT WAS *GREEN EGGS AND HAM*.

ROALD DAHL INVENTED ABOUT **250 NEW WORDS.** MOST APPEAR IN *THE BFG*. HIS LANGUAGE IS KNOWN AS GOBBLEFUNK.

Cinderella was first published by French author Charles Perrault in 1697.

Prince was 6 ft 7 in (2 m) tall!

The record for the most people balancing books on their heads was 998 people in 2012.

In 1921 *The Tale of Peter Rabbit*, by Beatrix Potter, was published in braille.

We hope you enjoyed our book!

GLOSSARY

We are a robot army. We can do any job. We are on page 112.

ALGAE
Simple plants that have no true roots or flowers.

ARCHAEOLOGIST
An expert who finds out about human history by digging up things and studying them.

ARCHITECT
A person who designs buildings.

ARTIFICIAL INTELLIGENCE
The science and study of building machines that have the ability to learn and think in human-like ways.

ASTEROID
A rock that floats in space, orbiting the Sun.

ASTRONAUT
A person who has been trained to travel and work in a spacecraft.

ATMOSPHERE
The layer of mixed gases that surrounds a planet.

ATOM
A tiny particle of matter. Atoms are composed of smaller particles: electrons, protons, and neutrons.

BLACK HOLE
An area in space where gravity is so strong that nothing can escape it, not even light.

BLUBBER
The layer of fat between the skin and muscle of whales and other animals.

CANYON
A deep valley with steep sides, often with a stream flowing through it.

CARNIVORE
An animal that eats meat.

CARTILAGE
A tough, flexible tissue that covers the ends of bones in joints.

CONSERVATIONIST
Someone who promotes careful management of the natural environment.

CULTURE
The inherited ideas, beliefs, values, and knowledge of a group of people.

DRONE
An unmanned aircraft or ship that can navigate without human control or beyond the line of sight.

ELEMENT
A substance that cannot be broken down into simpler ingredients.

EMPIRE
A group of nations that are ruled over by a leader or government.

EXOPLANET
A planet that orbits a star other than the Sun.

FAULT
A line of weakness or a crack in Earth's crust along which a plate of rock can shift or slide.

FOSSIL
The ancient remains of an animal or plant that lived thousands of years ago. A fossil may be animal remains, footprints, or a plant, preserved in rock.

GALLEON
A large sailing ship of the 15th to 17th centuries that was used either as a fighting or merchant ship.

GLADIATOR
A man in ancient Rome who was trained to fight to the death in the arena.

GRAVITY
The force that attracts objects toward one another. It is also the force that attracts, or pulls, objects toward the Earth.

Let's rock! For the music, go to page 158, and for the stoney kind, check out page 56.

What's a rain-making laser beam? Find out on page 106.

HUMANOID
Looking like a human being.

INFLATABLE
A small rubber boat that is inflated with air.

LABYRINTH
A maze of paths or passageways in which it is difficult to find one's way or to reach the exit.

LASER
An intense, focused beam of light used for communications, cutting, welding, astronomy, surgery, and much more.

MAGNET
A substance or object that attracts certain substances, such as the metal iron.

METEORITE
A rock from space that reaches Earth's surface without burning up in the atmosphere.

NANOBOT
A microscopic robot.

PAPYRUS
A tall water plant that was used as paper by the ancient Egyptians.

PARTICLE
A tiny part, such as an atom or molecule, that makes up matter.

PHARAOH
The title given to the rulers of ancient Egypt.

PHOTOPHORE
A glowing organ found in certain deep-sea fishes.

PLANETARIUM
A building where the movements of the Sun, Moon, planets, and stars are projected onto the inside of a domed ceiling.

PLATEAU
A large area on land or under the sea that is mostly flat, usually with lower areas around it.

PROSPECTING
Searching for gold.

RAIN FOREST
A tropical forest with tall, evergreen trees and a high annual rainfall.

RAPTOR
A meat-eating dinosaur that ran on its hind legs.

SAUROPOD
A gentle, plant-eating dinosaur, often very large, with a long neck and a long, whip-like tail.

SEISMIC
Relating to, or caused by, earthquakes or earth tremors.

SPACE JUNK
Objects such as satellites and material discarded or lost from space stations that remain in space after they have been used.

SPECIES
A particular group of living things, whose members look similar and breed together.

SUBMERSIBLE
A ship that submerges and operates under water.

TOUCHSCREEN
A touch-sensitive display screen on a computer or electronic device.

TSUNAMI
A huge wave produced by a seaquake or undersea volcanic eruption.

Lucky we have a glossary. Even I learned some new words in this book!

OLD TIMES

There's gold on page 32. Take me there and find out who the Aztecs and Incas were.

INDEX

I need to get this parrot back to the rain forest. Let's find our way back to page 80...